North of Porter

Kirkland Ciccone

Published by
Strident Publishing Ltd
22 Strathwhillan Drive
The Orchard
Hairmyres
East Kilbride
G75 8GT

Tel: +44 (0)1355 220588
info@stridentpublishing.co.uk
www.stridentpublishing.co.uk

Published by Strident Publishing Limited, 2015
Text © Kirkland Ciccone, 2015
Cover art and design © Ida Henrich

A catalogue record for this book is available from the British Library.

ISBN 978-1-910829-00-4

Typeset in Optima by Andrew Forteath | Printed by Bell & Bain

This book is dedicated to Portia Penelope Pinkerton.
Get well soon, Endless Empress.

PROLOGUE
SPLAT!

The day Porter Minter became an orphan was the happiest of his life.

He stood back and watched as an angry mob tossed his parents from the roof of the tallest building in town. And he waved goodbye as they fell.

Most people wouldn't laugh as their parents became pavement pizza.

But Porter laughed for weeks afterwards.

That summer changed Porter more than he could have imagined:

It was the summer of The Strike, the riots, and the disappearances.

It was the summer of snow and storms and starvation.

It was the summer of The Alien.

DO ANDROIDS DREAM OF EMMA PEEL?

The Factory was part of the city, woven into the very structure of its structure.

It was an unsightly and invasive blot on the horizon, the dominant view from every single window of every single house on every single street. But it was also strangely comforting; a reminder that, no matter what happened, The Factory would always be there for people. The Factory was wealth, protection, reliability, community and history.

The Factory was heart and life and everything.

Then it all stopped.

And that's when Porter Minter arrived, stuck in the back seat of a crappy car.

*

"This place looks like a warzone," Porter Minter sourly declared as snatches of his new home shot past the car window. He could barely bring himself to look at the whizzing world, because it was all so depressing. The little town of Castlekrankie looked like Germany after the blitz, Hiroshima after the bomb; or worse…Cumbernauld one minute after it was built.

"You'll love it here." Ma smiled through chunky bright pink lips. Her make-up always looked terrible, as though she had been dragged face-first through the cosmetics section of Planet Pound.

"You have no choice but to love your new home," Pa laughed snidely.

Porter stifled a strong urge to reach over and punch his

father's barrel neck. But Pa was right, of course. Porter silently contemplated his grim fate as his parents cackled demonically from the safety of the front seats. They weren't taking any chances with their son – they'd removed the handles from the back of their car so he couldn't escape.

The family car was a prison on four wheels.

"Why did you have to bring me here? I actually liked my last school. I had friends. We could have settled down for the first time in our lives," Porter shouted from the back. But his parents ignored him, choosing instead to talk at him about how great everything would be at his new school. They wanted him to make lots of new friends, especially friends with lots of money.

They needed people of influence and wealth for their plans to work.

"We're going to be rich here in Castlekrankie," Ma said with a big pink smile.

"How do you know?" Porter spat back at her. He couldn't hide his revulsion.

Pa chose to answer his question, which in itself was a rare thing:

"This wretched dump is the biggest UFO hotspot in the country."

Porter felt a familiar darkness wrap around him, an ache that his medication couldn't shift. And he had lots of medication to pull him out of his gloom.

For Porter's parents to end up rich, it meant innocent people would end up poor.

~~I hate them both and I want them to die.~~

"I swear I'll tell the police everything!"

Pa Minter turned the wheel of the car violently, his knuckles glowing from the effort. "Oh I doubt it, my generously-proportioned pilfering progeny!"

Porter scowled, because he recognised an insult when he heard it.

"And why is that?"

This time it was Ma who answered, and there were lipstick traces in her a sweet voice, the same voice she'd used to sing nursery rhymes to Porter when he had been a child. She could sing him to sleep with that voice. She could make him laugh with that voice.

She could make him cry with it.

"Do you like your nice expensive Dr Martens?"

Porter said nothing. There was nothing for him to say. Everything would be used against him. He expected this to happen. He wouldn't give his parents the satisfaction.

"Do you like your Harris Tweed coat that you begged Santa to bring you? Aren't you glad I didn't decide to throttle you with your lovely Burberry scarf?"

Now Pa joined in with comments of his own:

"Do you like using that lovely diamond-studded watch on your wrist to tell the time?"

"It's made from real silver!" Ma added spitefully.

"But it isn't as expensive as that handbag you carry around with you!"

Porter pulled his black Dolce & Gabbana handbag closer to his chest, nearer his heart, and turned his nose up at his parents.

~~I hope they crash this car into a wall and smash through the damn windscreen!~~

"Yes," Porter said aloud, his voice wavering slightly. "Yes I like my things."

"Then shut your mouth and do as you are told!"

Porter opened his mouth to say something suitably cutting, but then thought better of it. He felt sick with anger, the sort of repressed rage that bubbles on the inside and stays in the stomach, until something happens to release it.

That would come later.

The car slowed and Porter looked at his brand new house.

It was a block of flats, clean and new, but a block of flats.

"We had an actual house with an actual garden before we moved here!"

The car turned and made its way into a communal car park. Neither parent replied to their son, so Porter sighed, and waited for them to let him out of the car.

They didn't let him out.

It took a few minutes for Ma to get out of the car, because of her immense weight, and Pa had to drag her out by her legs. Then they slammed the door and left Porter inside, alone and trapped. Porter didn't bother yelling for help, because he knew no help would come. This was his punishment for speaking out against his parents.

When Porter looked around, he saw his Ma's face pressed against the grimy window of the car. Her skin left greasy stains on the pane of glass.

"This is what you deserve" – her breath misted her face – "and if you don't do as you're told...I'm afraid you'll be abducted by aliens – just like your brother!"

*

Her threat was received understood.

Because Porter knew fine well his older brother hadn't been abducted by aliens.

He knew his parents were liars.

He'd known since the day he'd found his brother's dead body stuffed inside a suitcase.

PUNY EARTHLING,
WHO WILL SAVE YOU NOW?

Rain drummed against the windscreen, the soundtrack to a miserable night locked inside a smelly old car. Porter closed his eyes and pretended he was inside a spaceship, a small shuttle powering through space, skimming stars, a flight across eternity.

Then someone knocked on the window.

Porter opened his eyes to see a face peering through the glass.

It belonged to a little boy, at least twelve years old; his hair was so messy he could have been turned upside down and used to mop up a dirty floor. The little boy kept shaking his fringe out of his face, to enable him to see clearly, and at that moment he could see only Porter being miserable in his car prison. His eyes were blackened with tiredness.

"You're silly," he giggled.

"And you're a nosy little brat," Porter snapped at the kid.

"What are you doing?" the boy asked with a mighty shake of his hair.

"I'm having a party with my invisible friends."

The boy shook his hair again and looked around the inside from the outside.

"I can't see anyone."

"That's what invisible means you scrawny twit!"

"Oh."

Porter wanted to yell his frustration, but in space no-one can hear you scream. Captains of starships never had to deal with this sort of nonsense; if presented with a problem, they simply photon-torpedoed it into space dust. This humiliation,

Porter thought, was the only thing Castlekrankie had to offer.

"Could you please let me out of this car?" Porter pleaded with the boy.

"I'm not supposed to talk to strangers."

"Yes, that's great advice and I completely agree. But I'm stuck in here and my parents won't let me out."

The boy shook his messy hair but said nothing. He seemed to consider Porter's appeal for freedom. But he didn't have the luxury of time in which to make his decision, because the lights from lampposts dotted around the road had flickered into life and made the street glow sickly green. It was now Officially Late.

"My mum locks me out of the house too," the kid said in a voice thick with sadness. "But I like it, because it means I can search for my dad."

Porter felt his shoulders hunch, which was either a reaction to what the little boy had just admitted, or cramp from being stuck inside a car. He had instinctively known as soon as he saw the boy look through the car window that he came from a poor family. He had the look of someone who had been left to his own devices for too long.

It wasn't just his uncut hair or the tatty red tracksuit jacket stained with the remains of various dinners, blotched with what looked like ketchup. It wasn't the little blue inhaler he kept in his left hand. It wasn't even the dark around his eyes, a harshness Porter could see despite the evening murk. Mostly, it was the emaciated skin that covered the rest of his face: the boy had the air of someone who hadn't been fed properly for a long time, the complete opposite of Porter who, despite his occasional trips to the back of the car, lived somewhat lavishly.

"Honestly," Porter assured him, "I look like a weirdo but I'm actually a nice person."

And that was enough for the boy. Porter waited to hear the familiar click clink of the car door handle being pulled, and then the door opened wide. A cold blast of wintry wind hit Porter. He gasped aloud at the sheer intensity of it.

Despite the cold, it felt amazing to finally be able to stretch his legs and emerge into the world, even though it was unfamiliar territory.

A painful spasm moved up from Porter's toes to his back, the result of having been trapped in the car for too long.

"Thank you for setting me free, young man!"

"Young man?" The boy's tone was almost incredulous. "I'm only twelve!"

"I'm fifteen years old, but I'm far more intelligent than most teens my age."

It was a proud boast from Porter but not one *anyone* took remotely seriously.

"How come your parents locked you in the car?"

"They think they're punishing me, but they're just making me angry."

Porter slammed the door of the crappy car with enough viciousness to make the old automobile shake. ~~One day,~~ a voice said rebelliously in his left ear, ~~I'll smash it up.~~

The car, however, fascinated the boy with the messy mop of hair.

"So you can't get out unless someone opens the door from the outside?"

"Ma and Pa removed the handles and rigged the car so it only opens from the outside, or with a special key. And I don't have that key."

"But what if someone wants to steal it? They can get inside from the back door!"

Porter laughed resentfully.

"Who would steal that collapsing heap of crap?"

The boy agreed, and then he shivered. It was late and cold.

"You should get home," Porter said sympathetically, and then he added:

"Thanks again for rescuing me. I'm honestly grateful."

The boy shook his head and then took a deep puff of his inhaler.

"My name is Alfie. What's your name?"

"I'm Porter Minter."

"I'll see you at school tomorrow!"

~~I'm not going to school! You can't make me!~~

"Bye, Alfie."

Alfie shook his hair, turned and ran towards an enormous tower block, the same building Ma and Pa had entered earlier after locking Porter in the car.

Porter stood still, momentarily distracted by the glorious shapes his breath curled into, and then he decided to get inside out of the cold. He turned, lifted his genuine Dolce & Gabbana handbag out of the car, and moved towards the block entrance.

It was only when Porter reached the intercom system that he realised he had no idea which number to press. His parents hadn't told him where he lived!

~~Tossers!~~

"Tossers!"

UPPERS, DOWNERS,
AND CANDY BARS

When people live their lives in a horrible area, they try to find ways of making their surroundings less unpleasant. Class is far more desirable than trash; hence giving a classy name to a trashy place makes things a little more tolerable for residents.

So when the people of Castlekrankie were asked to name the enormous tower blocks that desecrated the skyline, they leapt at the opportunity. They felt important for the first time in their lives, so everyone took their task very seriously. The local authority made only one stipulation: *that the people choose the name of these ugly old tower blocks from a list of significant people*. The list of names provided was of people who had, in their own way, made a significant mark in history.

Porter had been living in his new flat for barely a week when someone knocked on the front door, asking him for suggestions. He voted for Churchill Tower, because Winston Churchill had won a war against the odds and Porter himself felt like a war veteran.

But everyone else in the building chose Beckham Block, named after their favourite celebrity footballer and underwear model.

Oh well.

*

The pills were lined up in a neat row, just waiting to be rinsed down with a glass of water. Porter looked at them suspiciously, and then he looked at Ma, who met his questioning glare head on. She handed him a glass filled to the brim, so it sloshed as Porter lifted it.

Each pill was a different colour, and each colour represented a different problem.

"What are all these for?" Porter asked steadily.

"You know what they're for," Ma snapped at him. She wasn't in the mood for defiance or backchat. It was an important day for her son. It was his first day at a new school. The last thing she wanted was for him to draw attention to himself.

The pills were control and security.

"But they cloud my brain and make me feel like crap!"

"They help you cope," Ma said, her voice silky. She couldn't fake concern very well, because every time she lied her right eye twitched.

Porter didn't fancy spending another day locked in the car, so he placed his hand on the table, slid it along, catching the pills one by one, until they rolled off into his palm. He warily took the glass of water with his other hand, a ritual he was used to, and swallowed his medication.

The rainbow tasted of chalk.

*

Porter was six years old when he had his first nervous breakdown, though he refuses to this day to call it a breakdown, preferring the term Existential Crisis.

He went to bed dressed in his paisley-patterned pyjamas, as he did every single night. But when he woke up the next morning…he couldn't move! He lay there, completely conscious but trapped inside his head. Porter tried to scream, but his mouth didn't obey. He couldn't do anything but slouch on his bed, tears pouring down his face. The tears were the only things that kept him locked into the world, because he could feel them…and taste them.

Ma had to drag her son across his bed until his body flopped off the mattress. The ceiling moved along with Porter, and then the floor tilted, replacing the roof. He fell with a thump! But

Porter didn't cry out in pain. He simply didn't move, couldn't move. He just stared vacantly, not letting his body respond to anything that didn't interest him.

But Porter could still *hear* everything:

"Get up you stupid boy! Stop this nonsense at once or I'll put you in the cupboard!"

(In the days before the car without handles, there had been the cupboard without light.)

"Do as your mother tells you!" Pa yelled from the bottom of the stairs. He sounded irritated, which made sense because he always sounded irritated when he wasn't making money. A small part of Porter perversely enjoyed all the attention.

"I think something's wrong with him," Ma's voice projected away from Porter. He couldn't really see her, but the patterns on the carpet were fascinating. Rings, continual circles, and Porter's brain focussed only on the circles, until he fell deep into them.

"We can't take him to the hospital! He might tell them about his brother."

"Help me..."

"What? Did you say something? He said something!"

What happened next was something Porter would never forget as long as he lived. It was the one thing that he could piece together from that day; the moment that made the memory:

Pa lifted him up in his arms, sat him down on the bed and slapped him hard across the face. The pain brought Porter back with a cry of surprise. His father was level with him, eye to bloodshot eye. Porter saw worry in them. And what, even then, he recognised as a hangover.

"Your brother is gone."

"Gone," Ma agreed enthusiastically, though her eye twitched as she said it.

"But it wasn't our fault."

"It was the aliens!"

Twitch, twitch.

"The aliens were too powerful, son."

"The aliens took him away in their shiny silver spaceship."

Porter said nothing. It all made sense. His parents talked about aliens constantly. They were alien hunters! The most amazing job in the world! Of course his brother had disappeared with the aliens.

"Do you want a candy bar?" Ma asked. She had an enormous box of candy bars that only she was allowed to open. This was a big deal, because she never shared!

"Yes please," Porter replied, suddenly finding his voice again.

*

Porter found his voice, but he didn't find the suitcase for another two years.

And in that time the Minters moved houses, changed names, became different people with the same job: hunting aliens. They were everywhere! They were in shops, on the streets, in buses, at school.

A life looking for aliens is stressful for a child.

No wonder Porter needed his pills.

CRACKED PAVEMENT BLUES
AND CREEPY MYSTERIES

Porter met Alfie on the way to school and they exchanged phone numbers. Porter had a sneaking suspicion that he might need help escaping Ma and Pa's car again, so Alfie could prove useful in that regard. Porter also liked the idea of having a new friend. And, even better than that, Alfie hadn't said a single word about Porter's black handbag, which was slung over his right arm. He simply puffed from time to time on his inhaler.

The first day at a new school wasn't a daunting experience, not for Porter, because he had experienced *many* first days at schools around the country. This was just another new school that would soon be replaced by another school, and then another and so on. Alfie, however, was a boundless bundle of energy. He was so excited that he hopped about at Porter's side with sheer gusto, talking about everything without any thought or filter. He wore a backpack, a horrible luminous yellow thing that clashed with his red tracksuit. And it was Alfie's sartorial mishap that made Porter blurt out:

"You wore that same tracksuit last night!"

Alfie stopped in the middle of the street, his energy ebbing away.

"My mum can't afford to buy me new clothes," he said, his sleepy eyes blinking heavily.

~~You're an insensitive twitmonkey and I will soon be free.~~

"I only meant that you aren't wearing school uniform."

~~Improvised on the spot! Well done...but I will still soon be free!~~

"I don't like school uniform!" Alfie laughed in relief, the

inhaler up at his lips.

"I look like a debt collector when I wear uniform, any uniform whatsoever."

*

The rest of the journey was spent in silence as Porter was led by Alfie towards Castlekrankie High School. Along the way Porter took in his surroundings with growing disgust. The town's architecture was dark and warped, a bad drug dream from the nineteen sixties, with new bits grafted onto old bits, council-issued white window frames at odds with the homes they let light into, and rows of shops with metal shutters in place of doors. This wasn't a town rich with a swollen middle-class, the sort of people Porter's parents needed to survive. It was a town on the brink of a nervous breakdown (or perhaps an Existential Crisis).

Porter understood exactly how the town felt about itself.

*

After a few minutes of walking, Porter pointed forward at the horizon. There was something on the edge of his eye, large and squat; it flared with heat as it belched thick and sickly trails of twisted black smoke out of its chimneys. The thought of breathing that black smoke made Porter feel sick to the point he had to restrain himself from gagging.

"What the hell is that monstrosity?"

Alfie peeked out from his hair and nodded grimly.

"The Factory," he said softly as the cold made his breath come out in wisps, reminding him to fetch his inhaler from his pocket. "It's where my dad used to work. They make pies. Haven't you heard of the famous Marlowe Meat Pies?"

*

Porter quaked at the mere thought of those pies. He had gone vegetarian to avoid eating them. Those so-called scrumptious pies had about ten percent meat in them and ninety per cent animal debris. Porter remembered a time when he innocently tipped a pie upside down only to see grease pouring out of the sodden crusts. Ma had forced him to eat every bit of it regardless, greeting his tears with laughter.

Never again would he eat a Marlowe Meat Pie.

*

"Yes," Porter stifled the urge to purge, "I've heard of Marlowe Meat Pies."

"That Factory is where they came from before everyone went on strike."

"How long has it been going on?"

"It feels like forever," Alfie said sadly.

Porter was about to say something else when he suddenly cried out in pain.

"Hurry up!" Alfie called at him once he realised his new friend had simply stopped.

"I can't!" Porter gasped. He trembled visibly, his eyes wide with terror.

"Why?"

Porter didn't reply with words. Words weren't enough to describe his feelings at that moment. Instead he motioned at the pavement where he stood, allowing Alfie to follow until he saw the cause of the problem.

There was a crack on the concrete, a long thin line between the kerb and the corner.

"I have Obsessive Compulsive Disorder!" Porter announced with embarrassment. "I'm sorry but I can't step on a cracked pavement!"

*

OBSESSIVE COMPULSIVE DISORDER is a mental health

condition suffered by millions of people across the world. Symptoms include obsessive activities, thoughts, feelings, and compulsions. These compulsions range from mild to severe. Simple actions such as washing your hands can suddenly take on a frightening significance. You can't go to sleep without making sure every single switch in your house is off. Little tasks you take for granted suddenly become overly complicated.

For Porter it was the cracks beneath his feet that terrified him more than anything. Because sometimes, when he looked at them, he felt he could slip and fall between those tiny little cracks…never to return again.

*

Porter and Alfie eventually got to the school doors, two large glass walls which hissed open as soon as they approached, but Porter was still shaken by his experience with the cracked pavement. It was all he could think about! He hated cracked pavements; and he hated spending so much time thinking about his phobias and why they upset him so badly.

~~Cracked pavements remind you of your cracked brain. You might as well be on the other side of a burst dam, or a gaping gulf of no return. But I can see out of the crack.~~

Alfie, however, didn't care about silly things like broken concrete.

He had other worries – real worries that Porter couldn't understand.

From the outside, Castlekrankie High School appeared new and modern, the only contemporary building in an entire town of old red bricks and dirty cracked streets. Footsteps echoed on smooth marble flooring, and Porter instinctively let out a long satisfied sigh now that he was away from the broken ground.

His joy was short-lived.

As the glass doors slid open, they left a group of teenagers free to leave the other side of the school. They were an average group, boys and girls together, dressed in the ghastly purple uniform of Castlekrankie High School, except one boy (their leader?) who wore a bright red jacket. ~~Is the red jacket their school uniform? Yuck. Red makes us look fat!~~ The group sauntered past Porter and Alfie. Snatches of their conversation reached Porter's ears: something about a surprise party for a girlfriend, and the need to keep it secret. Then suddenly, as though the group of teens had only just realised Alfie was in their presence, they came to an abrupt halt. It was almost cartoonish.

That's when they started screaming and shouting things at Alfie and Porter. Insults! They yelled the worst most horrible words in the world. Some were so creative that Porter didn't quite understand how to physically enact them. One of the little gang, a freakishly tall boy, placed his face inches away from Alfie's just so he could spit on him. The spit was thick and creamy, and Porter nearly gagged. "You're a scab boy!" the tall bully shouted. "You'll always be a dirty little scab boy!"

The bunch of hooligans were so pre-occupied with attacking Alfie that they didn't even stop to mock Porter's handbag, which was usually the first thing bullies at school noticed when Porter enrolled for classes. He would be bothered if he weren't so angry:

"What *is* your problem?" Porter seethed, irate that anyone, let alone an entire gang, would laugh at his new friend for no apparent reason. He looked over at Alfie.

"I might not like cracked pavements, but I can certainly crack some faces!"

Alfie pretended not to hear a single word. He absorbed their hate, took a shot of his inhaler, and casually walked away.

Either that or his thick hair had grown into his ears, blocking any sound from entering.

"What are you doing?" Porter snapped at his little friend.

"Did you hear what they called you? Aren't you going to fight back?"

The little boy weaved through the pupils walking around him, and still he ignored Porter. A harsh electronic tone buzzed through the building, carried by strategically placed speakers.

Porter had been in enough schools to know that this was the sound of the first bell.

"You need to learn to stand up for yourself!" Porter yelled as Alfie disappeared into the crowd. And then Porter had a *moment*, realising that he sounded like a damn hypocrite, after all…the first time he'd met his scruffy new friend, he had been locked in the back of a car as punishment for standing up for himself.

"Damn," Porter said as Alfie turned a corner, his shadow looming large against the wall as he walked away. And then Porter was alone, wondering whether he should chase after his new friend. But he didn't.

Instead Porter walked idly along the corridor without a single care for his surroundings; he knew he wouldn't be at this school for very long. He simply moved where the signs took him. He needed to find English class, but the signs had a different plan for him.

They took him to something downright disturbing.

*

It was a large cork notice board, so big that it obliterated the cream-coloured wall at the end of the adjoining hallway. Posters of shifting colour and size were stuck to the board. Each encapsulated the hopes and dreams of anxious parents. The posters had faces of children and teenagers on them. Each poster had one word above each face:

MISSING. MISSING. MISSING. MISSING. MISSING.
MISSING. MISSING. MISSING. MISSING. MISSING.
MISSING. MISSING. MISSING. MISSING. MISSING.
MISSING. MISSING. MISSING. MISSING. MISSING.

*

Porter stood alone in the corridor, wondering what had happened to all the missing of Castlekrankie.

MISS HAPPY LEMON WASHINGTON

Whenever Porter moaned about being bored, or having nothing to do, his parents would simply tell him to get out and get himself a hobby.

For once in his entire life Porter did as his parents commanded.

And what was this exciting new hobby?

Making crank telephone calls!

Porter's favourite target was a dreadful woman named Miss Happy Lemon Washington.

*

Everyone in the country knows about Miss Happy Lemon Washington!

She's one of the most famous stars on children's television. Everybody who watches *Happy Lemontown* will have witnessed the vivacious Happy Washington in action. It's like witnessing a crime – a crime against television.

The incurably giddy Miss Happy Lemon Washington is a vision in bright yellow chiffon, with a voice that could kill a cave of bats from ten miles away. She easily hijacked the show after her introduction, quickly turning it into a showcase for her dubious singing talents. Despite being fiftyish, Happy is *always* the beautiful princess on the show. The actors all have to pretend to be in love with her, because no-one gets to be as beautiful as Happy Washington. Every actress under the age of forty disappeared off the show soon after Happy made her first appearance. Kids who loved Sally Strawberry, Katie Crumbly, and Mrs Owlish soon came to accept their effete replacement.

But the best thing about *Happy Lemontown* is...
...it's filmed in Castlekrankie!

*

"Bonjour," Porter said in a ridiculous French accent, because he didn't want anyone to track him down using voice-recognition technology. (Yes, his parents had made him paranoid about simple phone calls.) "Could you please fetch Miss Happy Lemon Washington for me?"

The voice on the other end sounded weary, and her sigh was long and loud. "Can I ask who is calling?" There came a slightly anxious pause.

"Tell her it's the doctor. I'm phoning from the clinic. I want to discuss her test results. It's really bad because...and I know you won't spread this...*Miss Washington* has a severe and incurable case of Ugly Syndrome."

"There is no such condition as Ugly Syndrome," the voice said quickly.

"If Miss Washington doesn't speak to me, I'm going to leak her real age to the press. I'll tell everyone that she's really fifty-eight and not twenty-three."

"..."

"Oh yes," Porter said beautifully. "I know her real age!"

There was a long silence from the other end of the phone, and then a quick hushed discussion between two different voices. Porter knew for a fact that the receiver had been covered up to prevent him hearing the conversation.

Then another voice spoke from the other side.

Porter's heart rushed with joy and anxiety.

It was Miss Happy Lemon Washington!

"I will crush you," she hissed, "I will find you and crush you under my heel."

"That isn't a nice way to speak to your number one fan," Porter cackled wildly, enjoying his moment of triumph over a despised enemy. He enjoyed this far too much, and he knew it had to stop...but fighting with Happy was the one thing that allowed him to let off steam. He kept so many secrets, and sometimes when he felt ill with rage, these phone calls were the only thing that let him feel normal again.

(It often occurred to Porter that the anger he let loose on Miss Happy Lemon Washington should really be set free on his parents.)

"Why do you always smile?" Porter asked. "People who smile all the time give me the creeps. It isn't natural. You look like an axe-murderer on TV."

He winced as a noisy shriek of indignity burst through the speaker and into his ear.

"One day," Happy Washington squealed, and Porter could almost imagine her smiling that sunny smile as she spat the words down the phone, "I'm going to find you. And when I find you, I'm going to get my revenge. No-one disrespects the star of *Happy Lemontown*. Don't you know who I am? Don't you know how many people my show employs in this town? Without me there would be no Castlekrankie..."

The sound of a key being inserted into the front door brought Porter back to his surroundings. He looked at the phone and quickly pressed the button to kill off the call. The sound of Miss Happy Lemon Washington's maniacal laughter was killed off too.

The phone rang again. Porter didn't even get a chance to put it down.

"Hello?"

"It's me," said a little voice.

~~Not Happy Lemon, thank goodness.~~

It was Alfie! He sounded upset, his voice shaking badly.

But two sets of loud footsteps were moving slowly up the hallway towards Porter's bedroom, where he was imprisoned. He couldn't be caught with his phone. Every muscle in his body tensed with unhappiness at the idea of this little bit of freedom being taken away from him. Porter's bedroom was extremely lavish with all the comforts a boy of his age could want: an ornate French-style double bed carved from the finest mahogany sat in the middle of the room, complete with the finest fluffiest pillows to rest Porter's head. The television on the wall *was* the wall. There was an en suite bathroom and a well-stocked refrigerator. But the one thing Porter wasn't allowed was a telephone.

Ma and Pa didn't know their son had a secret phone.

In the past they had discovered and smashed many of Porter's phones.

"Where are you, son?"

"I need to go," Porter said in a hushed but fearful voice. "I'll see you at school!"

"Can you see the lights?"

~~What lights? I can't see anything? It's dark in here, Porter!~~

"I'm sorry but I really need to go. You can tell me about it tomorrow."

"I can see lights, Porter…and I think I heard someone scream…"

The phone was shoved under the opulent Hungarian goose-feathered pillow, and then Porter lay back on it to muffle any intrusive sounds. He breathed a happy sigh, thankful that he had managed to hide it so quickly. He sat on his bed, waiting for the inevitable.

Then the bedroom door flew open to reveal Ma and Pa. They wore identical expressions of distrust.

"Did we hear you talking?" Pa asked in a perilously low voice.

"If we heard you talking, that means you have a phone!" Ma chipped in. "Phones aren't allowed in this house."

"Phones are used by aliens to read our thoughts!" Pa said.

"Your brother had a phone…" said Ma, "…before the aliens

took him away from us!"

Talk of his brother riled Porter, and undid the relaxing effect of his crank calls.

"I don't have a phone. And I would climb out the window and run away if I didn't live on the eighteenth floor of a high-rise. I'd do anything to get away from both of you!"

Then he said something else that really infuriated his parents.

"And I talk to myself because I like to have conversations with *honest* people!"

*

That little bit of insubordination earned Porter another night in the back of the car. Worse, he didn't have his phone, which was still underneath his pillow. So he couldn't contact Alfie and ask him to let him out. So he sat there, shivering in his pyjamas, watching the street through dirty glass.

~~Maybe Alfie will wander by and get us out of this damn car.~~

"I'll see you tomorrow at school," Porter said brightly to his grimy reflection.

But Porter wouldn't see Alfie the next day at school.

In cutting off his call, Porter had inadvertently said his last words to his new friend. Alfie would soon become the subject of the next poster to be pinned up on the school bulletin board.

TEENAGE GIRL POST-PARTY

The distant noise of the party carried across the night; the uplifting sounds of joy and laughter, echoes of a triumphant birthday. Most people in the surrounding homes tolerated it because there was little to celebrate these days, especially for the young.

Emily Jackson, still giddy from her surprise party and all the surprise cocktails, tottered down the street with an awkward grace. The heel of her left shoe had snapped clean off, so her walk was heavily unbalanced. But she didn't care. Her sister would probably care – they were her heels that Emily had pinched for the party – but Emily felt as if she could float in the air with joy, because Darryl Miller had asked her out on a date! She had known he liked her – had always known – and she liked him too. He'd told her the party was his special present on her birthday. He'd even wanted to walk her home, but that would have been a step too far. Emily didn't want her dad to know anything about Darryl or the party.

The supple, freshly-set snow was a lovely addition to the world around Emily; it was almost fairy-tale in its beauty. She wore a red parka jacket, which had been another gift from Darryl, the vibrant colour as bright as Darryl's hair. He liked her, he'd given her a party, and he'd worried about her feeling cold on the way home!

Emily had promised to return his jacket at school.

She stopped in the middle of the street and did a little twirl of joy.

"I have a boyfriend!" she squealed. The words were strange, and so she repeated them until they sounded right, "I have a boyfriend and his name is Darryl!"

The entire street was dark, except for a random flicker of yellow light from a cracked lamppost. Outlines of cars, houses, and tower blocks were illuminated every now and again. But without the light they were simple shapes in the night.

Emily scowled at the shape of The Factory in the distance.

It ruined her night slightly.

"Give my dad his job back you scummy scabs!"

She pushed forward as a gush of icy wind cut through her. The red jacket protected her top half, but her bare legs (she wanted to show them off to Darryl at the party) nearly buckled beneath her.

"Why does the snow need to be cold?" Emily whined. It didn't matter though, because her house was only one street away. Soon she would be nice and warm under her quilt.

But it wasn't the cold that was chilling her. She had a strange sense that something was wrong. She couldn't *see* anything wrong, and yet her instincts disagreed; they wanted her to run as fast as possible, to GO HOME AND LOCK THE DOOR.

Emily pulled Darryl's red jacket tightly around her body and smelled his Joop aftershave.

Someone...or *something*...was following her.

Emily walked quickly, or as quickly as a sixteen-year-old girl with a broken heel can in snow, but not quickly enough. Her heart pounded in her ears as blood made noise. She faked calm for a few minutes and then broke into a travesty of a run.

Emily was halfway down a street, just across from Beckham Block, when her entire body lifted itself up into the air. It held her there for a few seconds, dangling in the grip of something incredibly powerful. She thrashed her legs and arms wildly in a bid to escape. "Let go of me!" she cried out.

But her voice sounded small, childish, terrified.

"Please let go of me!"

Something sharp pricked her neck, right beneath her hairline. She let out a cry of pain, though it wasn't actually painful. The arms encircling her waist twirled her around and hurled her with enormous power across the road. She saw the street spin and fly right at her face. It hurt. Everything hurt. Then something grabbed her again, slamming her onto the pavement. Something cracked. Pain blasted through her body. Agony! She screamed and looked up at a human shape, in front of her, moving quickly out of the gloom.

This was her chance to finally look at the face of whomever... or whatever...was trying to hurt her. And what she saw when she looked didn't make sense.

Two large oval eyes, unblinking, stared dispassionately down at Emily.

"Dad!" she croaked, hoping he would hear her from across the road. But her throat had been paralysed during the struggle, and she felt something dripping from her neck, down her back. She cried out again. Only a strangled gasp could be heard in the night, drowned out by the sounds of her party. She was now beyond fear and deep into terror.

Her hands gripped the red parka jacket and held it up, hoping it might bring her luck or protection. But the jacket was snatched out of her hands and torn into shreds, the ripped pieces thrown down at her as she begged for mercy.

"Darryl!" Emily screamed, praying for him to rescue her, her hero.

Something formed in Emily's confused eyesight, so strong it overwhelmed her blindness:

She could see lights in the white.

Red and blue, blue and red, they came closer and closer towards her.

And then she was gone.

TEENAGE RIOT REALNESS

It all started when Alfie didn't show up for school.

Porter felt slightly nervous walking to school alone, especially in a town he didn't know well enough, along a route he wasn't confident walking. He waited outside the door of Beckham Block longer than he ought to have, then decided to go to school.

The last thing Porter wanted on his second day at a new school was to be late.

He found his way down the street, keeping an eye out for familiar landmarks that he remembered from the previous day: an odd lamppost here or there, red graffiti on the wall of the church. Finally he spotted a large group of teenagers in Castlekrankie High uniform. Porter followed them until they led him to the school gates.

There was a ripple of wrongness in the air, an aura that something wasn't quite right. Porter felt it keenly. Something bad was about to happen.

It was the same feeling he'd had the day he'd opened the suitcase and found his brother.

*

Porter didn't last long in registration class, which was a relief because everyone ignored him. Not one person acknowledged him other than Miss Gorham, the teacher of History who looked like a relic from a bygone age herself in a jazzy cardigan and Louise Brooks bobbed hair. She asked Porter his name and he responded, "Here," and that was literally his one moment of interaction with another human being at school. But her voice was extremely irritating, and she enunciated words in a strange manner, leaving Porter clawing his face in dismay in full view of his new classmates.

"We HAVE a special LAST-minute guest speaker who has come to visit us, for WHAT reason I have NO idea but I'm SURE it's important since it WAS the headmaster who agreed to HAVE him here today."

"At least we don't need to go to Geography," a voice said to the east of Porter.

He turned to see a girl wearing…he frowned…an elaborate black hat and veil covering her face. ~~How odd,~~ his secret voice said. ~~Maybe she's going to a funeral after school?~~

But aloud Porter told her, "I think you need my medication more than I do!"

Before the girl with the veil had a chance to reply, the sound of a door opening distracted Porter, and he turned to see the special guest speaker entering the room. Porter raised an eyebrow, because it wasn't what he'd been expecting.

The special guest speaker was a policeman! An officer in uniform, with a truly rubbish moustache. He smiled and introduced himself to the classroom.

"I'm Officer Robert Hatfield of Castlekrankie Police, and I'm here to talk to you about your missing classmates…"

Porter felt weak with fear. For a second he was absolutely terrified Officer Hatfield had come for him; he'd spent many nights harassing Miss Happy Lemon Washington, and she'd promised to visit all sorts of vile retributions on him. Porter suddenly had vivid daydreams about being arrested in front of everyone in Class 5B, but this fantasy gave way to another powerful thought. His fear transformed into excitement as a new idea came to him, a plan to give him the freedom he desperately craved.

~~You could stand up, walk across the room, and tell the police about my parents…we could finally tell the truth about what they've been doing for years…I could get justice.~~

"I'd be free from them and that damn car," Porter said, muttering under his breath.

~~I would too! You just need to open your mouth and say the words that will set us free.~~

But before Porter could open his mouth to say any more words, he watched as everyone in the room, including Miss Gorham, *booed* the policeman.

*

After nearly ten minutes of jeering, catcalling, hissing, screaming, yelling and every other sort of heckling at the disposal of teenagers, poor Officer Robert Hatfield regretfully made his excuses and left the hostile atmosphere of the classroom.

Porter decided to take control of the situation and demand answers.

The answers, however, created more questions... unfortunately for Porter.

"He's a policeman," the girl in the black veil said, as though that explained everything.

Another angry voice called out:

"They're stopping my dad getting his hands on the damn scabs!"

"So the police are stopping people hurting each other... basically they're doing their jobs?" Porter said sarcastically. These people were stupid. Everyone was stupid.

"The scabs are stealing jobs!"

That word again. Porter had no idea what this actually meant, so he did what every confused schoolboy should do when they don't know the answer to a question: raise a hand.

Porter raised his hand... and amiably asked Miss Gorham: "Please miss, what *is* a scab?"

Someone jeered from the left side of the room:

"You should know!"

Another cried:

"You're a scab follower!"

Everyone laughed, but Miss Gorham smiled a peachy grin and nodded her head gracefully. She didn't want to allow disharmony to derail her lesson now that Officer Hatfield was gone. So she decided to humour the new boy and answer his question.

"A SCAB is a dirty LOWLIFE scumbag who goes to WORK when there's a general STRIKE. And we hate scabs, don't we class?"

Everyone in the classroom cheered; except Porter, whose mind was still fixed on the comments about him being a 'scab follower'. That and the fact that Officer Hatfield hadn't been able to talk about the missing teenagers. Porter really wanted to know why so many people were disappearing. He needed to hear the official explanation.

"If I can TEACH you ANYTHING," Miss Gorham said sagely, "it is that SCABS are SCUM!"

*

The harsh electronic three-note tone of the bell pierced the classroom and everyone sprang into action. Bags were grabbed, chairs were moved, and people left the room to head to their first classes.

Porter went to pick up his handbag, only to realise it wasn't where he'd left it.

"Please miss! Someone has stolen my Dolce & Gabbana bag!"

He couldn't lose it! It was too expensive!

Miss Gorham sighed and rolled her eyes at Porter's melodramatic ways.

"Kitty," she said in a preachy voice, "did you steal the scab supporter's bag?"

Porter turned and found the girl with the black hat and

veil holding his bag. It was unzipped and she seemed to be rummaging through it.

"Get your grubby hands off my luxurious designer handbag!"

"I'm sorry," Kitty Stomp – for that was her name – mumbled nervously.

"I can't believe you're trying to steal from me...in front of me!"

Kitty's eyes were wide with sadness behind the veil.

"I really can't help it. Please don't tell the policeman!"

But Porter wasn't easily pacified. He felt stressed and angry over how he was being treated, not only by his parents but by everyone at his new school. He still had no idea what was happening with Alfie. And now *this* silliness!

"I truly madly deeply can't help it. I'm a kleptomaniac."

Porter backed away, because he only recognised the word 'maniac'.

"I steal things," Kitty explained.

"Why?"

Porter caught a glimpse of knowledge pass in a glance between Miss Gorham and Kitty, an understanding that united them. But it wasn't to be explained to the new boy.

Not yet.

Kitty looked down at Porter's schoolbag and slowly, agonisingly, handed it over.

"I won't tell the police," Porter said.

"Thank you!"

Porter stretched out his hand.

Kitty was hesitant at first, and then she took it and shook it.

"You're weird," she said, as her free hand adjusted her black veil.

"*You're* weird," Porter replied.

"Let's be friends," Kitty added.

And just like that they became friends.

to:	Sir Hemmingford Higginson
from:	Professor Milo Wrathorga
subject:	The Sleepers

What is the meaning of this interference in my work? I am being harassed by General ███████████, who has for some reason taken exception to my methods. He says I am overstepping my authority. I really must have something done about this interference.

Yes I've had to perform ███████████ on the men, but they understand, as you do, that it is all for medical science, and I am doing good work here to cure them of their problem.

The General claims to have your support.

Is that true, old friend?

DEATH AND THE DAD

Porter and Kitty walked alongside the river that ran through the park, a vein on the surface of the skin. The park and the river had both seen better times. Porter couldn't take his eyes off the sheer amount of crap in the water: upturned prams, plastic boxes, old chairs covered in patterns that hadn't been fashionable since the '90s, and rusted lockers bearing the logo of a nearby factory.

"Wow," Porter said aloud. "If one man's trash is another man's treasure...then this place is full of riches. I'm surprised none of it has been pawned for cash."

Kitty, however, didn't seem to hear Porter's catty critique of the park.

Or if she did hear it, she didn't seem to care.

Instead, without looking at him, she asked:

"Do you want to meet my dad?"

Porter raised an eyebrow. He then raised a glass bottle of Coca-Cola to his lips and sucked through the straw. Acid rots teeth and Porter refused to drink fizzy juice without a straw. He hated the idea of having to go to a dentist and have someone rummage around his mouth. What if they hadn't properly sterilised their equipment? The last thing Porter wanted from the dentist was all sorts of diseases.

"Do I have a choice?"

"No."

Porter shrugged, slurped the dregs of his Coke, and threw the empty bottle over his shoulder. It hit the water with a very satisfying plop!

*

The two teens reached the Stomp family home: a lovely detached house with a garden, and a conservatory.

"I used to live in a nice big house like this," Porter remarked wistfully as he remembered his life before Castlekrankie; the past was a distant place, vague and as unreliable as his parents.

But Kitty didn't go into her house. She kept walking.

"Oh! I take it your dad isn't in the house?"

"No," Kitty called back. She moved faster away from Porter, who had to quicken his pace to keep up with her. They walked with determination and purpose, though the actual purpose was a mystery to Porter. He was just about by Kitty's side when she suddenly broke into a run.

"Oh no!" Porter whined indignantly. "Running is really uncool!"

"Follow me and I'll take you to my dad!" Kitty cried as she jogged further and further into the distance.

Porter tried his best and managed to keep up a steady run until he finally caught up with Kitty. Huffing and puffing, he looked up at where she had brought him.

"I'd like you to meet my dad," she told him with a slight smile.

Porter took in the iron gates in front of him and groaned miserably.

It was the graveyard.

*

The graveyard was devoid of actual living people bar a pensioner with a peaked cap and a dog chain, who walked past the church, followed by his nimble pet. Porter could only watch in horror as the man's dog – a pit bull terrier – peed on the grass beside the tombstone. The dog's owner didn't care and pretended not to notice Porter's horrified expression. Instead he moved away and entered the church.

"Someone needs to tell the parish priest there's a scummy

dog-walker letting his mutt pee over the graves," Porter fumed. He felt an attack of painfully hot indigestion, which may have been either the Coca-Cola or anger upsetting the delicate balance of his stomach.

"That dog walker *is* the parish priest," Kitty told him.

Then she hastily stopped and pointed down at a tombstone.

"Hello, Dad," she said cheerfully.

The tombstone remained silent.

Kitty nudged Porter, and he winced because the blow was quite painful.

"Aren't you going to say hello to my dad?"

Porter's face screwed up into a good impression of someone who had been forced to lick pit bull terrier pee off one of the dandelions that the graveyard greenery had in abundance. He couldn't bring himself to reply, because the situation was bizarre.

Eventually, after a minute, he managed to squeak:

"You can't be serious?"

*

It wasn't that Porter was unsympathetic; after all, he did carry his older brother inside a suitcase every time he was forced to move home. But he couldn't bring himself to talk to a tombstone, especially when it belonged to a man he didn't know, or hadn't met.

A man he would *never* meet.

*

Kitty had already opened up her rucksack, and rummaged around inside it until she found something important. This was clearly a ritual she had practised ever since her father's death. Porter watched in horrified fascination as the girl pulled out something for her father.

"Here it is!" she cried excitedly.

It was a can of beer.

Worse, it was a can of Special Brew – in Porter's view, one of the nastiest beers in the world.

Kitty caught sight of Porter's visible disapproval, and hit back with:

"It was his favourite!"

"You aren't going to drink that over your father's grave?"

"Oh it isn't for me," she laughed, "it's for him."

She pulled the ring and sprayed the can's frothy contents across the tombstone. It dribbled down the mossy stone and was swallowed up by the dirt, until the earth had drunk up the entire can of beer.

"I do this every week. He would have wanted it this way. A good can of Special Brew was his favourite thing in the world, next to me and Mum."

The two teenagers stood in solemn silence with their heads bowed respectfully. The snow started while they waited. To Porter the Castlekrankie snow was the coldest in the world. But it felt important to say nothing while his new friend grieved. Kitty's veil covered her face, but it couldn't muffle the slight sound of sobbing.

Porter thought of his brother and then he thought of Alfie.

He still had no idea what had happened to his other new friend.

More minutes passed by and the snow gained strength. It began to settle on the soil. Porter eventually mustered the courage to put a little motion into the motionlessness, because he didn't want to stay in the graveyard forever.

"Do you mind me asking you a question?"

"Fire away!"

"How did your father die?"

Kitty took a deep breath, because it wasn't an easy subject to discuss. She looked at the can of Special Brew before she gently laid it down beside the grave. Then she said in a voice that sounded as if it might break into either more sobbing or else hysterical laughter:

"He was an alcoholic."

Porter reached out to give his new friend an awkward hug, because he didn't know what else to do. She sniffled, trying to wipe away her tears, and then she asked:

"Will I come to your house and meet your parents?"

"No," Porter replied, and stepped away from Kitty. Talk of his parents reminded him that it was getting late. His curfew was severe and his parents would send him to the car (again) if he broke it. "I think it's time to go home," Porter announced, "it's getting late."

"You're right," Kitty said quietly. "There's the curfew too."

Porter was astonished when he heard that Kitty also had a curfew.

"Why?"

"The mayor announced it a few months ago," she said with a dramatic sweep of her arms. "There's an eight o'clock curfew because of the violence. The strikers have been smashing things up and looting shops, so the police are out afterhours trying to catch them. And there's also all the disappearances! People fade away in Castlekrankie…especially teenagers. If you're sensible, you'll get home and lock your doors."

Porter wanted to ask Kitty lots of questions about the town and the disappearances, but most of all he wanted to chat about Alfie. He knew something was badly wrong, he still felt it strongly. The idea gnawed at him, because Alfie had found him in the car and set him free.

~~He opened the car door and let us out after eight o'clock… which means Alfie was out after the curfew. Why was he out so late? And did he often leave his house after eight?~~

"I'll see you tomorrow at school. I'd like to ask you some questions."

Kitty smiled under her black veil. It was a nice smile.

"I'd like that a lot. You aren't as bad as I thought you would be, Porter. For a scab sympathiser, you're actually an okay guy."

~~What? Is that meant to be a compliment? Idiot!~~

"Thanks?"

Then they parted ways until the next day, leaving behind an empty street.

It wouldn't be empty for long.

ROID RAGE

Vinnie Durkin loved his girlfriend Katie so much that when she announced her pregnancy, he got down on one knee before her family and asked her to marry him.

He felt slightly guilty later that night when he had to punch her in the face. He tried to tell her it was for her own good, because she had forgotten to add gravy to the potatoes, which were far too lumpy anyway. Vinnie couldn't stand Sunday Roast (even though it wasn't Sunday) without the proper trimmings, and gravy was too important to get wrong. But he hit her because he loved her so much.

Vinnie decided to leave Katie alone in the house for a while, just so she would have time to think about her mistake. "Mistakes are for the weak," he told her as he left their flat. On the way out, he stopped and checked himself in the hallway mirror, admiring his tight body and gloriously muscular torso. *The body of a champion*, he thought with satisfaction, *and everyone is jealous of it.*

*

Roid Rage was the only shop in Castlekrankie dedicated to selling the finest food supplements. Nutritious dietary aids in the form of powder and pills, the sort of stuff gobbled up by fitness fanatics and bodybuilders. It had a small gym built into the garage on the corner of the premises. The fitness freaks loved the gym, because there they could share health tips and illegal steroids; the sort of nasty stuff that warped bodies and brains.

And Vinnie loved his steroids nearly as much as he loved himself and his motorcycle.

Vinnie zoomed past The Factory, slowing only enough so the crowds outside could experience the glory of his KTM 1100. It was bright red, or as he told everyone: "the colour of danger." He revved the engine and laughed at the pathetic tramps standing outside with placards. They all had the same thing on their signs: SCABS GET OUT! WORKING WAGES FOR WORKING MEN! OUR JOBS, OUR LIVES!

Vinnie caught sight of another group of men filing past the gates under armed police escort. The men and women with signs weren't happy and they didn't try to hide their anger. A small riot broke out between the strikers, the scabs and the police. Vinnie slowed the motorcycle further and stared at the men rushing through The Factory gates: scabs trying to escape the mob outside. It was the night shift, so clearly the scab scum had attempted to sneak in so they could avoid the picket line. They had failed. Someone – a policeman Vinnie thought – threw a punch, starting a chain reaction that became a riot.

"DUMB SCABS!" Vinnie screamed as he revved his bike.

Someone – a random scab – looked over at him, and Vinnie caught an angry frown.

Come on, Vinnie thought furiously; *come ahead if you think you're hard enough!*

The scab reconsidered and turned his attention to the angry strikers.

Vinnie roared triumphantly, grabbed the handlebar, and accelerated hard.

That's when the astronaut ran past him.

Vinnie swerved around the white figure.

"Twat!" Vinnie yelled angrily.

He could have dismounted and battered the nutter in the white costume for nearly killing him, but he had to get to Roid Rage before it shut for the night. His chest was tight with anger, his veins ready to burst, and he desperately needed a good workout to get rid of the excess energy. And, most of all, he badly needed his special vitamins to make his workout…work.

It was only when the astronaut faded into the distance that Vinnie realised the suited figure had been trying to *stop* him riding away.

*

Roid Rage was located in a small industrial estate on the east side of Castlekrankie, an area filled with units rented out to small businesses. These businesses were far busier than Roid Rage, and yet for some reason Roid Rage seemed to be able to pay its rent on time every month. The owners of the various units knew fine well how Roid Rage generated its extra income, but said nothing.

The last person to speak out against Roid Rage's late night activities – the owner of Castlekrankie Van Hire – had arrived the next day to find his vans had been stolen overnight.

Vinnie Durkin had done it as a favour to his friend.

But he wasn't paid with money. He was paid in steroids, the good stuff.

And as he pulled up in the car park of Roid Rage, he stole a glance over at where Castlekrankie Van Hire had once resided. The memories made him smile.

*

Vinnie snarled when he saw the metal firmly shuttered over the entrance to Roid Rage. He was too late and now he couldn't have his workout. Worse, he would either need to wait for more steroids, or phone someone and collect some for later.

This is Katie's fault! Damn bitch. She did this! She made me late!

Vinnie turned and made for the car park but stopped, startled, when he realised there was someone standing in front of him, blocking his way back to his KTM motorbike. He laughed, at first, because he thought the astronaut had followed him down the road. But it wasn't the astronaut, although the person in front of him was dressed just as outlandishly. He didn't have much time to study the figure, but caught a glimpse of wide, black, unblinking eyes and grey, dull skin.

"Are you an alien?" Vinnie chuckled.

But it was gone as suddenly as it had appeared.

Something sharp pierced Vinnie's left shin – sharp and quick. He twisted around to see…a shape…weaving through the car park, ducking and dodging behind cars. Whatever it was, it was extremely fast.

Something giggled in the night.

Then it moved towards Vinnie, blurring and fading into the darkness. He punched outwards, his muscles rippling and tense, and managed to land a devastating hit. But his knuckles connected with something hard. Bone cracked in Vinnie's hand and he howled as pain shot through him.

He tried to swat away the weirdo but something grabbed his arm, twisting it violently. Vinnie knew it wasn't a joke, or some idiot in a costume. He had read all about the mysterious freak who abducted teenagers and knew they were never seen again. He tried to pull away but his arm broke under the assault. Vinnie screamed again. The pain from his two wounds was so bad that Vinnie almost fainted.

Almost, but he was tough. Too tough to simply give up.

The giggling resumed, and then a voice spoke aloud. It sounded like a hissing whisper. He couldn't quite see where it was coming from, but it was very close by. For a moment Vinnie was sure he could see a pair of green eyes blinking at him, blazing with the sort of bright colour that wasn't possible from human eyes.

We are one are we one no we aren't one but we must be one to be the one…

I must walk this world and kill again with hands…human hands…large, strong hands!

WE ARE NOT ONE!

Vinnie used this moment to attack his attacker.

He jumped up and launched a powerful kick at the shape in front of him.

The pain in his useless arm caught Vinnie by surprise again, but it was replaced by a pained yelp from his assailant. Vinnie turned and ran for his life, staggering wildly across the car park towards his motorcycle.

He was halfway out of the car park when something smashed into him from behind. It hit him so hard that it instantly ruined his perfect body, and his last thoughts as he lay dying were of Katie and her stupid lumpy gravy.

Then he was crushed to death.

MEMORANDUM

to:	Sir Hemmingford Higginson
from:	Professor Milo Wrathorga
subject:	The Sleepers

The ▮▮▮▮▮▮▮▮ has been compromised by stupid soldiers who constantly interfere in my experiments. How am I supposed to help if I cannot use these men as guinea pigs? They knew the risks and I am not a sadist, regardless of what people say about me. You must order ▮▮▮▮▮▮▮▮ to step down and allow me to continue with my work.

I have put the men into ▮▮▮▮▮▮▮▮.

And please make sure my funds are topped up otherwise I will have no means of paying for equipment and people to test my theories out on.

These men deserve peace of mind.

BUCKFAST ROGERS
IN THE 21ᵀᴴ CENTURY

As soon as Porter crossed from the outside of his flat into the hallway, he was instantly roped into helping Ma and Pa with the family business. It had been a long and strange day, a stressful one, and now he was going outside again. He couldn't be bothered.

"No," he snapped, arms folded across his ample chest. "I'm not doing it!"

"You need to contribute some of your time to our work," Ma replied angrily.

"NO!"

"Yes," Pa hissed, "or you'll spend the next year in the back of our car."

Porter crossed his arms defiantly and struck a fashion-magazine pose:

"I'll report the both of you!" he yelled at his parents.

"Are you going to phone Childline?" Ma laughed.

"No," Porter shot back, "the police!"

Pa launched across the hall and, with a swing of his hand, slapped Porter hard across the face, sending him onto the floor. He then dragged his son off the floor and pushed him into place in front of the hall door, where he stood rooted in fear.

The three of them remained there, in the intersection between the living room, the kitchen and the storeroom where the Minters kept their equipment. But the storeroom – in reality an oversized cupboard – contained something else, something Porter thought about every single day:

The suitcase with his brother's mummified body, which was firmly locked away out of reach.

"Go in and get the machine," Pa commanded, as he cracked his knuckles.

"I can't go in there," Porter cried out, his voice on the edge of hysteria.

"Don't look at the suitcase! Just edge past it and get the machine!"

Porter swayed on the spot, trying to move but unable to work his legs into motion. He really didn't want to go into the storeroom, because as Pa had correctly guessed, that would mean passing his brother. But Pa quickly lost patience:

"GET IN THE CUPBOARD AND BRING OUR EQUIPMENT OUT NOW!"

"Ungrateful little bugger!" Ma smacked the back of Porter's head as he opened the cupboard door. The slap was painful enough, but Porter felt keenly the sting of something else – fury, perhaps, and if not fury them something close to embarrassment. He clenched his teeth, because he didn't want to cry in front of them. He couldn't show weakness.

~~Don't you dare cry! Tears are for wimps. Never give them what they want!~~

"Okay," Porter said whilst rubbing his scalp tenderly. "But don't ask me to help you again. I can't deal with it anymore."

Pa snorted derisively. "You aren't as strong as your brother," he muttered under his breath.

But Porter heard – and felt – each word. And as he ventured into the dark of the cupboard, he held his breath and reached out towards a metal handle.

He prayed he wouldn't accidentally touch the suitcase.

*

The special equipment used by alien hunters who aren't actually alien hunters isn't especially complicated. There was only one machine Ma and Pa needed: a modified version of an everyday device millions of people use in their gardens, a piece of heavy-duty equipment that had helped them make lots of money in the past.

It was heavy and awkward. The Minters needed their son to help share the weight of the machine to the elevator. But Porter ended up taking most of the weight alone, because his parents were immensely lazy and too busy chatting about money. So he pulled, and pushed, and dragged the machine awkwardly through the front door of the flat to the outside corridor, until he reached the elevator. Drenched in sweat, feeling completely gross, Porter finally manoeuvred the machine into the small carriage.

Hello, said the elevator with perfect enunciation, *please speak the floor number and...*

"Ground!" Porter snapped.

He was exhausted, but the night's work had only started. The doors of the elevator slid shut, cutting him off from his parents, but Porter was grateful to have a few minutes of peace without them. He would have to drag the machine to their car, of course.

And then the spirit of the elevator asked Porter an obvious question:

What are you doing with that lawnmower?

"I'm about to spend the night making crop circles with my parents," he replied.

The double doors slid open to reveal the ground floor of Beckham Block.

Have fun mowing the lawn, the spirit of the elevator said with a hint of synthetic laughter.

*

The Minters drove ten minutes down the road through what felt like a ghost town. Porter marvelled at the effectiveness of the curfew, which had brought the town to a standstill. He used his time in the car to think about everything that had happened to him over the last few weeks. There was an atmosphere of violence in the air, a horrible all-encompassing wickedness that was inescapable.

Was it the strikers?

Was it the scabs?

Or was it something else?

The car stopped. And the door without a handle opened to reveal…

*

"This is the most exciting hill I've ever seen in my life," Porter said sharply.

"It *is* quite exciting," Ma replied, her eyes wide with excitement. "And technically it's virtually a Munro, which is almost a small mountain."

"I was being sarcastic!"

But Ma didn't hear her son, because all she could see was money stretching as far as the hill was wide. Porter realised that his parents were planning something spectacularly nasty for the people of Castlekrankie. But he had no idea what, because they told him very little these days. He stood in the cold, watching little flakes of snow weave beautiful patterns in the night. He didn't know what his parents wanted of him.

"It's bloody freezing!" Pa moaned.

"Get the lawnmower out of the car!" Ma yelled. "That'll keep you warm!"

Pa looked directly at his son.

"You heard what your mother said! Get the lawnmower out of the car!"

"Whaaaat?! She told *you* to get the lawnmower, not me!"

The Minters gave their son a death glare and he trudged past them to the car, submissive. He opened the back and pulled out the lawnmower, making sure it crashed noisily onto the tarmac at the bottom of the hill.

"Ooops," Porter smirked.

But The Minters were too busy setting up the grand scheme to care about their son or the noise.

He stood at the bottom of the hill, shivering in the cold as they started the lawnmower. It made no sound whatsoever, not one grind of the engine could be heard; instead the machine purred away softly, a noiseless marvel, cutting into the grass.

*

How do you make a noisy old lawnmower into a silent cutting machine? Some people tend to confuse power with loudness, but Pa Minter discovered a nifty secret method for muffling the rattling engine of his broken industrial lawnmower. And if you asked him, he would tell you it was a four-stroke masterstroke of genius, a moment of brilliance of which only he was capable! There was no way he could use a lawnmower at night without a way to quieten it; secrecy was the literal thin line between success and poverty.

And how did he achieve the dream of a silent lawnmower? Pa Minter filled the engine with custard!

*

"Pass me the custard, son!" Pa instructed as he prepared the mower for work.

"This will never work!" Porter sneered. He wasn't in the mood for this nonsense.

Ma reacted to his insubordination by slapping the back of Porter's head again, causing him to yelp in pain and surprise. She was rapidly losing patience with her bratty son.

"Pass him the custard or you'll be put in the car!"

Porter gave his mother the same death stare she'd given him earlier, except with added raised eyebrow. He then slunk away to collect cartons of cheap custard, the gloopy gross substance the Minters swore by, handing them over to his father. But as he did...he found himself mutinously dreaming up various ways of getting revenge on his parents.

"Nobody realises that custard is one of the greatest miracle substances in the world," Pa said as he tore open the first carton. "Custard can do everything!"

"Can custard get you a likeable personality?" Porter said with a grin.

Ma swiped at him but he ducked out of the way of her palm.

Pa finished pouring the last of the custard into his lawnmower and then, with a smirk, powered the machine up and waited for it to live.

It roared.

And then went improbably quiet.

"I win again," he said with his eyes fixed on his son.

*

Pa spent the entire night mowing patterns into the hills. These were not normal hills; they were bright red, the colour of the rare heather that grew on their slope. The patterns carved were strangely random, sometimes circular, mostly crisscrossing into neat languages only he understood. The night was long and Porter found himself slipping off into sleep, but he forced his eyes open because he didn't want to sleep in the back of the car (yet again). He remained perched on the bonnet, sometimes sneaking a look at his parents engaged in their work.

Porter's head again bowed to sleep, but he threw it back, refusing to let go.

The sun was coming up.

His parents had been mowing for hours.

When Porter opened his eyes to look at their handiwork, his line of sight caught something else, something up on the hill, far in the distance looking down on them.

It was an astronaut.
Porter nearly fell off the car in astonishment.
The astronaut waved at him.
And then turned and disappeared.

STOMP THE KLEPTO

Kitty Stomp had never been a perfect example of a well behaved child. She'd been a thief from a very young age, successfully snatching Sadie Gleeson's favourite Bratz doll from right underneath her nose. But Kitty had loved that anorexic doll despite it having a mutated mushroom in place of a head. She'd known as soon as she'd laid eyes on it that she had to have it. Nothing would stop Kitty getting what she wanted in life.

Nothing, and no-one!

But there was one person...a man...who had what it took to take what Kitty had!

Her father somehow discovered her stash of stolen goods and he wasn't happy.

Kitty knew he would never tolerate this idiosyncrasy in her behaviour.

The result was a climactic bedroom confrontation.

*

"I can't help it!" Kitty wiped tears away as her father loomed large over her. His hands gripped the headboard of her single bed, close enough for his daughter to see little bitty corpuscular veins under the skin.

"You *have* to stop yourself." His voice was calm, as it usually was even when he was angry. Releasing the headboard, Kitty's father wandered around her bedroom until he found a rather plump beanbag. He finally decided to sit, because he wanted to look into his daughter's eyes. Mr Stomp was a tall man, gangly and ungainly, so sitting down on a bag made him look ridiculous.

"I've tried," Kitty said imploringly, "but there's something in me that makes me take things…things I don't even want…and the feeling is so good, Dad."

She went quiet before adding:

"I think I'd die without that feeling."

She looked at her father and suddenly felt a sense of relief. He wasn't angry with her, could never be angry with her. He was the best dad in the world. Somehow, against the odds, Kitty's father saw the truth of his daughter's life and he spoke it:

"I work hard so you can have everything you want. What you're doing isn't necessary, it's an addiction and you can fight it. And you can win!"

Kitty felt many emotions in that moment of closeness; what her father said resonated deeply – he *was* a hard-working man who made sure she got everything she needed…and this truth explained the sudden guilt Kitty felt, because in that moment she knew she didn't need to steal from anyone anymore.

Everything she'd ever wanted and needed was already in her life.

"I'm sorry, Daddy!"

"No more stealing," he said as they embraced.

"No more stealing," she repeated.

*

But she'd lied.

The Great Strike of Castlekrankie happened only a few months after Kitty's bedroom intervention. The Factory suddenly turned against the town. The pies on the production line just stopped. Everybody lost their job and the money that came with their work. The first thing people did was head to the benefits office, but cutbacks from the recession meant the money for families was a pittance.

And for the first time in her life, Kitty was encouraged to steal.

At first it was small things like fruit and vegetables.

But she soon learned how to steal more and more, just so that her family could eat.

With her addiction unleashed, Kitty quickly turned her bedroom into a junkyard.

This came at a terrifying price:

Kitty's father developed an addiction of his own.

*

Kitty sat on the very edge of her father's bed, trying her hardest to be brave, because her mother had broken down and her brother was too busy playing on his old Xbox.

"It's an addiction," she said of the empty glass bottles scattered around the room.

Her father was lost in a slurry world of booze and frustration.

"You can fight it."

The workers had been crushed in the uprising against the supreme alliance at The Factory. And, in a moment of spite, they had made everyone redundant.

"And you can win!"

*

But she'd lied. Again.

ALIENS IN CASTLEKRANKIE

Porter went to bed a grumpy fifteen year old boy and awoke the next day sixteen years old...but still very grumpy.

With everything that had happened to him since arriving in Castlekrankie, he'd almost forgotten his birthday! He ran around his bedroom to study his appearance in the full-length mirror. His pyjamas were decorated with fourth-Doctor-Who Tom Baker's toothy face repeated infinitely, but what Porter was really checking for was signs of age on his face.

"Thank God," he sighed in relief. "I don't look old."

He threw open his bedroom door and made for the living room where he would sit and hatewatch *Happy Lemontown*. Then he'd get ready for school. He had a special day of snooping planned, and time was of the essence!

What Porter didn't expect was to find his parents standing outside his bedroom with a birthday cake in their hands. They were dressed as though for job interviews.

"Did aliens abduct my parents and put you two in their place?" Porter cackled.

Ma sang *Happy Birthday*, or a version of *Happy Birthday*, with every note reached and a few added that were off the scale. Each syllable in the song was massacred by Ma Minter, and for a moment Porter felt she was singing the song for herself and not him.

Porter hadn't expected them to buy him a birthday cake. It was a large cake version of a Dolce & Gabbana bag, with thick black icing and a marzipan buckle affixed atop the icing belt. This wasn't just a cake; it was an expensive sculpture.

The Minters led their son into the living room so he could get his present. It sat on the corner table beside the enormous flat-screen television, and it was wrapped in green paper, complete with a meticulous red bow.

Porter regarded the package suspiciously, before lifting it up and tearing the paper.

His parents had bought him the same bag that his birthday cake was based on!

"Wow!" he gasped. "I don't know what to say."

Pa glowed triumphantly, his good taste confirmed.

"It cost us over nine hundred smackers!"

Porter knew the bag was expensive as soon as he studied the stitching and the ornate logo branded into the fabric. He couldn't believe his parents had done this for him.

"Thank you," he said quietly.

~~They're trying to buy you off! Don't be weak. Refuse their filthy bribe.~~

"We worked overtime," Ma said – her usually harsh voice now a soft, pleasing tone.

~~They worked overtime. You know what that means don't you?~~

Porter didn't know how to react and for a moment he felt a rare kinship with his parents. His good mood didn't last, for the room filled up with familiar music from the title sequence of a horrible TV show.

Happy Lemontown was on and in this episode Miss Happy Lemon Washington was trying to find the ideal dress to fit her for the grand ball. But before it, she had to dance with a group of man-sized teddy bears. She was nearly as bad a singer as Ma.

"*Don't be a square,*" she sang, "*be floppy!*"

"It's your favourite," Pa said amiably, his yellow teeth exposed in a weird smile.

Porter fled the room to get ready for school.

Ma and Pa got to work as soon as he left. It would be an important day for them.

Kitty, complete with black veil and hat, was even more excitable than normal when she met up with Porter. She ran past the red-brick bin cellar, which jutted out of the side of Beckham Block, connecting each bin chute with each kitchen. Porter waited anxiously at the glass front entrance for Alfie, but he knew the boy wouldn't be coming to school. Never had Porter felt this powerless as he waited uncomfortably outside the doors, just across from the scary talking elevator.

"Ohmygoddidyouseethenews?"

"Hello, Kitty," Porter said pleasantly. "It's my birthday."

"Happybirthdaybutdidyouseethenews?"

"Unfortunately I didn't see the news, but I did get a glimpse of Happy Washington."

Kitty took several deep breaths before reaching that lovely little calm moment she rarely visited. Then she told Porter what she'd seen on the news:

"A woman on an early morning jog found crop circles up on the hills! Real, proper, actual crop circles that weren't there the day before...and everyone believes aliens are trying to communicate with us."

Porter sighed.

"Did the jogger look like an astronaut?"

Kitty frowned. Or at least Porter thought she frowned; the veil made it difficult to see. She laughed and replied, "No! She looked like a jogger."

This didn't solve the mystery of the strange spy on the hill.

"Do you want to know something else really weird?"

Porter didn't answer. Kitty was going to tell him regardless.

"The news team found empty cartons of custard near the hill. They think the aliens ate custard. Isn't that funny? We have a custard-eating alien from outer space in town!"

They both laughed as they walked to school, but for very different reasons.

*

The alien hysteria was even worse at school. The air was buzzing with excitement and disbelief as everyone talked about the crop circles. Every single teenager had an imagination, and it turned out that in Castlekrankie...the adults were as imaginative as the teens, because even the strikers were ignoring The Factory to visit the crop circles.

Porter could see crowds moving up and down the streets, past the school, in the direction of the hills. When he got to the gates of Castlekrankie High, he was astonished to find banners draped over the iron spikes; large cloth sheets of different colours with scrawled words on them:

ALIENS ARE WELCOME IN CASTLEKRANKIE
BUT SCABS AREN'T!

TAKE US TO YOUR MOTHERSHIP!
SCHOOL IS BORING!

BLOW UP THE FACTORY WITH YOUR
DEATH RAY!

Porter was amused to find that some pupils had left cartons of custard by the signs. He was about to head into school when something zoomed down the main road – the same road he had travelled down the previous night on the way towards the hills.

"It's the Crapmobile!" Porter yelled.

"What?" Kitty cried.

"My family car. I call it the Crapmobile. Follow me!"

And she did.

The two teenagers climbed a few white picket fences – appropriate in the strike-ridden town, Porter felt – in order to reach the hills quickly, but they weren't quite quick enough to prevent the press conference starting. The crowd heaved with spectators of differing ages, some of whom hadn't bothered with school. They were excited to see something in their town that wasn't related to The Strike. Suddenly anything was possible. The world was no longer flat. The crop circles had changed everything.

Police officers were scattered throughout the crowd, making sure there wasn't any trouble. Their uniforms marked them out as an intrusive force, but for once they weren't necessary. Porter couldn't sense any tension whatsoever. He felt strangely sick, because he had a feeling he knew what was about to happen. Pushing his way forward, he finally made it to the front of the scrum.

"...and do you honestly believe we have been visited by aliens?"

"Oh yes!" a familiar voice said happily.

Porter felt his insides bubble as the sickness overwhelmed him.

~~You forgot to take your medicine today!~~

"Shut up!"

~~You can't silence me forever. This town is full of craziness. I belong here!~~

"Not only have we been visited by aliens, but I think they're trying to talk to us."

Porter looked up at the two people who were the subject of the press conference.

Ma and Pa waved at the camera, drawing cheers from the packed crowd.

And Porter finally understood why he'd been brought to Castlekrankie.

to:	Sir Hemmingford Higginson
from:	Professor Milo Wrathorga
subject:	The Sleepers

You can't do this to me!

I will not let anyone interfere in what needs to be done for the good of the men.

My experiments are a success. If you withdraw my funding then I'll need to find people who will be receptive to what I'm trying to do. Please don't do this to me!

SALESMAN FROM ANOTHER WORLD

Porter didn't stick around for the rest of the press conference. He couldn't stand around while his parents lied to everyone, giving them a sense of hope where none was justified. Ma and Pa stood with their heads held high, giving a good view of their hairy nostrils, and told everyone that an alien had abducted their loved ones. More than that, Ma and Pa knew how to communicate with the alien. They could – in theory – send a message to the fleet which, they assured the crowd, was orbiting the dark side of the Moon.

"We have vast experience in dealing with aliens," Pa told everyone.

Those in the crowd were mesmerised by the strange duo in front of them. They had a shared charisma that seemed to swell in situations like these ones.

"We can bring back your missing children!" Pa added, with a persuasive smile.

No-one but Porter heard his mother say something under her breath:

"For a small fee, of course."

And that was all Porter wanted to hear before he stormed off. Kitty didn't follow him, because she knew from his reaction that he wanted to be alone. Porter was angry that his birthday had been tainted. ~~You thought they loved you because they bought you a bag? You're a bigger idiot than they look!~~ He was irate with his scummy parents for using the grief of families in order to make money. They were evil. ~~Yes they are evil and they should be punished for what they've done.~~ Worse, they were clever and would probably find at least a handful of gullible people with money to burn.

He passed a familiar face on the way out of the crowd.

"Officer Hatfield!"

Then, louder:

"Robert!"

The policeman who had been booed in Porter's classroom recognised him instantly, and he smiled warmly. He was in his official uniform, which was pressed to perfection. Porter noticed these little things, because he hated un-ironed clothes as much as he hated cracks in the pavement.

"I didn't know policemen were paid to watch fraudsters at work?"

Officer Hatfield removed his police hat and rubbed it on the edge of his elbow. He raised a suspicious eyebrow at Porter's comment.

"Fraudsters?"

Porter felt slightly remorseful, because as much as he hated his parents and the way they bribed him with lavish gifts, he knew he couldn't tell the truth about them. He had been instrumental in their lies and trickery. To report them was to report himself – he couldn't do it.

"They're being interviewed by journalists about alien abductions!"

Officer Robert Hatfield suddenly went quiet, as though deep in thought:

"Do you think these two people can get the missing teenagers to come back?"

And Porter suddenly realised one important thing, something that gave Officer Hatfield a life outside his duties as a policeman. It was far bigger than The Strike and The Factory. It explained not only his gullibility, but that of the entire town of Castlekrankie.

Someone close to Robert Hatfield had disappeared.

"Who was it?" Porter asked.

"My son," the policeman said in a voice brimming with devastation.

"When did he vanish?"

"Four months ago."

"My friend has gone missing," Porter said in understanding. "His name is Alfie."

But Officer Hatfield wasn't listening.

*

Porter couldn't wait to get back to his bedroom. He ignored the stupid spirit of the elevator as it taunted him for giving in and not using the stairs. But it wasn't the only voice that taunted him.

~~Your parents will ruin these people as they ruined you and your brother.~~

Please select a floor or you will stay here all day. I can wait. I am an elevator.

~~Dozens of people have gone missing...people your age... people like Alfie.~~

"You know which floor I want to go to," Porter said pointedly at the spirit, "so just take me there and shut up. I can't deal with more than one weird voice speaking to me!"

You have got such a bad attitude! By the way, you look older today. Is it your birthday?

~~Tell the elevator to shut up or I'll press its button and give it a migraine.~~

Porter grinded his teeth until the elevator doors opened. He ran out and headed down the corridor towards his flat, towards some kind of safety. It was all too much and he needed to get his medicine before his head exploded.

The pills were neatly laid out on the shiny faux-marble surface of the counter. Porter poured a glass of water and swallowed each and every pill in quick succession.

~~I will have my day! I cannot be stopped!~~

"Shut up or I'll blot you out forever and ever," Porter yelled irately at himself.

*

Time passed and the silence was soothing to Porter's ears.

He sat in his kitchen with a bag of crisps and some chocolate, relaxed and thankful that the voice inside his head had been quietened.

It didn't last.

A new noise broke Porter's tranquillity: it was one of the worst noises in the world.

It was the sound of someone knocking at the front door.

"I bet it's a damn door-to-door salesman!"

Porter launched himself off his comfy kitchen chair, moving towards the hallway, using the time in between to prepare at least a dozen vicious one-liners, phrases aimed at doing maximum damage to the salesman to ensure he would stay away forever.

He reached the door and opened it.

The words didn't come – *couldn't* come.

For standing in the doorway was a man in a grey spacesuit.

"Hello," a muffled voice said to him.

It was the astronaut from the hill!

HE'S A LAWBREAKING
HAPPY SLAPPER

Jordan Garrick, two hours late for his eight o'clock curfew, felt a familiar flush of excitement smoulder through him. His black hoodie was pulled tightly across his face to prevent CCTV cameras identifying him. Anonymity was important for his mission. He was ten points away from victory in The Games, and winning would mean finally impressing the Game Boy.

The thought of victory made Jordan quiver in anticipation. Or was it a shudder? It was freezing cold and Jordan felt the chill severely. The noxious stench of alleyway pee was powerful enough to impact on his nostrils, despite the pervading cold. He looked around his hiding place a skip – and wondered whether the bin men were on strike too.

He waited a few more minutes and then swiftly left his vantage point.

It was time. The ultimate score was finally in Jordan's grasp!

And then, he thought, I'll get home and tell mum I've been at the library, studying for my exams.

*

The Game Boy had ordered his gang of Gamers to play a brand new game. The Gamers lived for these games; each and every one spawned from the productive and poisonous mind of The Game Boy. The Game Boy, real name Rupert Carville, suffered from the worst acne in recorded history, a goth with a face only a mother could love...slapping. He never got the respect he deserved, or so he felt, and every day at school was a day of misery and laughter at his expense.

His skin, his hair, his clothes, his voice were all fair game for his classmates.

Rupert Carville's revenge on the world would be games of his own making.

His latest game was his favourite:

Smack A Smacky!

Ten points were awarded to each Gamer who could locate and slap a drug addict, or someone who looked like they might be on drugs. Castlekrankie had a lot of people who looked stoned or medicated.

For the points to be formally awarded, the assault had to be filmed on a mobile telephone and uploaded to the special online forum set up exclusively for The Gamers. At the end of the week, once all the entries had been uploaded, Rupert would look over them and award points. Being the Game Boy was a serious job and Rupert took it exceptionally seriously. Sometimes, when the Gamers were in a bad mood, they would try and buck his authority.

The Game Boy showed no mercy to anyone he suspected of treachery.

He had no idea Jordan was plotting his downfall.

*

Jordan had observed the druggie from a distance. It felt like hours, but in reality only forty minutes had passed, even though they were agonisingly long minutes, as though the snow had made time decelerate. The druggie was staggering around on the outskirts of the black forest, the dense trees that encircled Castlekrankie. Jordan never ever ventured into the forest. The idea of it freaked him out, because he'd heard rumours of people performing witchcraft under cover of night.

The druggie stopped and fell to the ground.

Jordan's fingers were exposed, the only part of him not

covered, and they struggled to make his mobile phone camera come to life. As he slid his index finger along his phone's glass panel, Jordan saw his fingers were bone white. The words 'bone white' stayed inside his head for a few seconds, because he liked the sound of them.

The druggie got back up and staggered again.

Jordan aimed his phone and ignored any ethics he'd had before joining The Gamers.

Then he struck!

The druggie had a dirty face. It was nasty and unshaven. His breath reeked too, and Jordan felt sick when he inhaled it. His revulsion made him angry, and his anger made him punch the druggie across his dirty face.

"Look what you made me do!" Jordan squealed in a high voice – high because it hadn't yet broken. "You're nothing but a gross smackhead!"

Jordan remembered that each hit had to be filmed so he could collect his points.

He was about to deliver another bloody blow when the druggie lashed out and swiped the phone from his hand. It swished through the air and smashed on the pavement.

But the druggie wasn't a druggie.

He was one of the many strikers from The Factory who hadn't eaten properly for days. Jordan howled in disbelief and bolted in the opposite direction.

The opposite direction was the forest.

The so-called druggie chased him, but was too weak to last long. He fell and caught his breath. He wanted to warn the boy not to go into the trees. He breathed out in ragged bursts, the cold searing his lungs, but he couldn't say anything.

He couldn't warn Jordan about the lights in the forest...the harsh lights...

*

Jordan felt an unpleasant array of new feelings and emotions replacing the giddy eagerness of earlier: *disgrace* was the strongest, quickly followed by *fear* of what his mother would say about him breaking an expensive mobile phone she hadn't yet managed to pay off.

"I'll be grounded for years!" he cried out at the dank forest around him.

Jordan stopped running and caught his breath. The forest had swallowed him whole, and he was hopelessly lost. His hand pricked something sharp as he ventured further into the trees. There was no blood on the wound, but he suddenly felt faintly lightheaded. He hated nature and it was all around him, cold and quiet and creepy. Everything around Jordan was withered and bony.

"Bone white trees," he said aloud.

Something caught Jordan's eye.

It flickered in the distance, completely at odds with the frosted white forest around him. He cupped his left hand above his eyes and squinted at what he thought were signs of civilisation. Lights meant electricity and electricity meant people.

"Follow the light and leave the forest," he said to himself, as if narrating his own computer game. But his voice wasn't steady. The tremor in it betrayed an apprehension he didn't want to admit to himself.

The light in the distance flickered and moved.

Jordan froze. The light was a beam and the beam seemed to be searching for something. It moved in a circle, then stopped, and moved again in a zigzag twist.

Someone moved towards Jordan, and for a moment he felt a surge of relief, a release from the tension he felt. He pulled his hood back and called over to the man just metres in front of him.

But it wasn't a man.

Jordan gasped and recoiled from the horror standing in the undergrowth.

It was dressed in grey, with large, black, round, unblinking eyes.

Jordan screamed in shock. Panic-stricken, he staggered backwards. His right foot snagged on a twisted root from an old tree, and he fell, tripped by a cliché. Jordan slammed down, his head smacking hard against a tree trunk. Then he drifted into a half-sleep, the sort in which everything is heard but nothing can be done.

He couldn't even move his fingers or toes. He couldn't speak.

Something laughed in the night. It was a vile little chuckle followed by a wheezy whisper...

This one might be suitable, it said harshly, and then it coughed.

Jordan felt weightless. An invisible force dragged him through the undergrowth, across the forest and into the darkness.

"Please...let me go..." Jordan pleaded.

We must be free and you are just one person *but we exist to destroy and hurt and kill but we want to walk again and feel again and kill again!*

Jordan felt a little strength return to his eyelids, which he opened.

He couldn't see anything. He began to cry silently, tears soaking wet trails down his face. He couldn't do anything and he couldn't see anything except...

There were lights spinning in the white, moving closer and closer to him.

And then Jordan was gone.

STRANGE VISITOR
FROM PLANET 5758

The escape capsule spun through the endless waste of space, lights flickering all around as warships, armed with the latest weaponry, unleashed death in a choice of colours. Green lasers were the trademark of The Alien From Another Dimension's war fleet. For some inexplicable reason it seemed to like the colour green. White was the colour of ships armed by The Alliance – the good guys who had fought The Alien for aeons.

Inside the escape capsule sat three men, one of whom happened to be JFK.

His ship having been destroyed in the laser bombardment, JFK was waiting for the fleet to rescue him.

But things weren't going according to plan.

JFK needed help. And it would come clutching a Dolce & Gabbana handbag...

*

The spaceman stepped forward and Porter stepped away.

He didn't know what to do, because it wasn't every day that a spaceman came knocking at the front door. Porter opened his mouth to speak, but stopped when he saw his face reflected in the surface of the astronaut's space helmet. His face stared back at him, returned but made bigger. Confusion eventually made way for curiosity, and the owner of the face watched as his expression ran the full gamut of emotions.

Porter also realised with distress that he had inherited his father's pointy nose.

Two gloved hands reached up and clasped the rim of the

space helmet.

"I swear, if you touch me I'll scream!" Porter puffed inadequately.

The hands removed the helmet to reveal…

A head spilling over with thick blonde hair and a smiling mouth full of square, perfectly-formed teeth, each of which gleamed flawlessly white.

The spaceman was in fact a teenager, probably a year or two older than Porter. Worse, he resembled the sort of male model that could only be seen strutting down a catwalk in Milan. So what was he doing wandering the hills of Castlekrankie inside a spacesuit?

"Hello," he said at last, "I come in peace. May I enter your primitive dwelling?"

"Do you promise not to throw me into a pit and wear my skin?"

"You aren't the one I want to kill," the spaceman said, his features suddenly sinister.

*

The spaceman was an absurd sight in the little kitchen. He sat on one of the chairs beside the table, momentarily distracting himself with the salt shaker, exploring its function. He examined it and suddenly seemed to relax, as though deciding the little plastic shaker wasn't a military threat.

"Your parents claim to be able to speak to The Alien."

Porter flicked the switch on the kettle and looked out the window to see a darkening sky. His parents still hadn't returned home and it was getting late. The hours had flashed past! Porter knew he wouldn't see his parents for the rest of the night. They were too busy being local celebrities, doing interviews and lying to the cameras.

"They're liars," Porter confessed.

"I saw you last night at the hills with your parents. Why

were they cutting the grass?"

"They were cutting crop circles in order to make people think aliens have landed."

"Why?"

Porter wanted to tell the stranger everything, but if he started…he might never stop. And there was so much dirt and nastiness lurking beneath the surface of the Minter family.

"My parents are con artists. They go from town to town stealing money from people."

The spaceman seemed troubled.

"So they can't communicate with The Alien?"

"They barely communicate with *me*!"

The spaceman paused to stare at Porter, which was an uncomfortable experience, but Porter had boiled a kettle full of water, so he had a weapon on hand if one was required. But for some reason he felt…safe.

Safe in the presence of a strange teenage spaceman.

"Who *are* you?" Porter asked.

"My name is JFK and I come from Planet 5758 in the constellation of Hypo Sot."

"Is Hypo Sot somewhere in America?"

JFK made a face as though he couldn't believe Porter had never heard of his home world, but he smiled and laughed. Somehow, strangely, they were becoming comfortable with each other. JFK seemed to sense no threat in front of him.

"Do star pilots drink tea?"

"Yes. And we eat biscuits too."

Porter had an abundance of biscuits in the cupboard (and underneath his bed), though it was difficult to reach them with all the cartons of custard blocking his reach. It took a few extra seconds to grab some nice cookies to share with his strange new friend.

"You've told me your name, but you still haven't explained what you're doing here."

JFK looked surprised.

"I'm here to save the world from an evil alien!"

Porter burst out laughing, because he couldn't take JFK seriously.

But JFK didn't laugh. He was absolutely resolute in his belief.

"If I show you my spaceship, will you believe I'm telling the truth?"

Porter suddenly stopped laughing.

MEMORANDUM

to:	Sir Hemmingford Higginson
from:	General Gary Henderson
subject:	THE PROFESSOR

It is with regret that I have to inform you what is going on with The Professor. Yesterday I caught him injecting untested chemicals into one of the soldiers, a man who couldn't object because he was deep in a coma. I know Project Dreamscape is still underway but that does not give anyone – not even a Professor – the right to torture people in the name of science.

He blames me for your disapproval.

He is out of control. He told me last week that he had been visited by an alien. I think the stress of his work has finally taken a heavy toll on his mental health. He isn't the man you once knew.

The Professor was observed outside the local school, offering money to the children if they would help him with his 'science project'. We have also caught him up at The Factory, offering money to the striking workforce for help with his medical tests.

I have told him in no uncertain terms not to do any of these things again.

He risks exposing us to the public. Our base is meant to be secret, as you know, and secrecy is of the utmost importance.

He has to be transferred out of here immediately.

THE SPACESHIP AT THE END
OF THE STREET

Porter wrapped himself in a fitted red jacket woven from the finest tweed. It had probably cost more than most of the strikers earned in a month when they worked at The Factory. But it kept Porter nice and warm against the frosty environment outside.

"Let's get the elevator," JFK said, "it'll be quicker."

"Oh no," Porter responded in anguish, because he knew what to expect.

*

The elevator doors were barely shut when the spirit of the elevator started taunting Porter's strange new friend. It was a verbal sparring that would not end well.

Where did your friend buy his stupid costume? the elevator said snidely. *I have to move people around this block all day and night...but I've never met Buzz Lightyear! Do you want to go to the ground floor or to infinity and beyond?*

JFK, eyes wide, looked unnerved. "Where is that voice coming from?"

"It's our friendly..." Porter spat the word 'friendly' out in the manner of someone who had eaten something dodgy, "... artificial intelligence, which runs the elevator. Here's a tip for you – it gets really annoyed if you call it a lift. So call it a lift!"

I am not a lift. I am an elevator and you will show me respect!

JFK moved swiftly to silence the disembodied intruder:

His right hand blurred as he unsheathed something from a hidden flap on his spacesuit and pointed it in the direction of the speaker from which the voice had emanated. Porter couldn't quite make out what JFK was holding in his gloved hand, but it vaguely resembled the some sort of toy ray gun that might have been plucked from the set of a bad sci-fi movie.

The ray gun spat a condensed flare that streaked from the nozzle to the speaker.

The elevator screamed and sparks of a thousand colours rained down on the teenagers beneath. There was a violent judder as the elevator went crazy in a bid to shake the intruders out of its interior. But JFK kept firing his ray gun.

The door slid open to reveal a brick wall, and then it slammed shut again. It kept doing this at a frightening rate, showing off what walls looked like between floors.

Porter screamed but his screams were drowned out by the spirit of the elevator.

Then normal service resumed.

The door slid open to reveal the ground floor of Beckham Block.

Porter ran outside, trying his hardest not to punch JFK for causing a mini explosion.

"I thought we were under attack from my enemy," JFK said by way of an explanation.

*

They were halfway down the street when Porter realised it was half past curfew. He wasn't too concerned though, because his parents hadn't returned yet, but there was always the chance that a policeman might mistake them for strikers…or that strikers might mistake them for policemen.

But every time Porter looked at JFK, he was reminded that absolutely nobody could mistake them for policemen or strikers.

He decided to use their journey to quiz JFK about his mission.

"So what are you looking for?"

"I'm hunting an evil Alien From Another Dimension."

"And it's somewhere in Castlekrankie."

"Affirmative."

"You were on the hill last night when my parents cut those crop circles into the grass. And you don't need to respond to that one, because I saw you in the distance."

JFK didn't reply.

"I assume you saw me today at the press conference and followed me home."

"I had to meet you and discover whether or not your parents were able to talk to extraterrestrial life. I'm the protector of this world and I need to stop any threat."

Porter rolled his eyes so much that he nearly walked into a lamppost.

"Tell me more about this alien."

"The Alien From Another Dimension," JFK explained, "is the one responsible for abducting all the teenagers in this little town."

Thoughts of Alfie, alone and terrified, flashed horribly through Porter's imagination and he suddenly realised that finally...perhaps...he had found someone who could help him track down Alfie.

"Why?"

"The Alien doesn't have a body like we do. It seeks to walk this world on two legs instead of hitchhiking inside a body. It wants to be whole and not just a fragment inside a human being."

JFK suddenly halted his stride and looked left to right. They were at an intersection of trees that Porter recognised even in the gloom of a dark summer night.

"This is the route I use to get to school," Porter said finally.

JFK didn't care about Porter's school route. Instead he suddenly burst into action, setting off down the road in the opposite direction from The Factory, south towards the school and towards the hills where Porter's parents had carved crop circles the previous night.

Porter checked for lampposts, then rolled his eyes again and chased after the strange teenage spaceman.

*

The journey to the spaceship lasted a few minutes. Porter had become accustomed to running, indeed he was now rather good at it. But it was late and the wintry embrace of the outside world was beginning to take a toll. Why was it always cold in Castlekrankie?

Porter was so deep in thought that he nearly crossed the road without looking.

JFK reached over and grabbed him by the shoulder.

"Get off me!" Porter snapped.

But JFK yanked Porter back onto the kerb, just in time to save him from a large black truck that powered past them.

The truck was massive, with colossal pavement-pounding wheels, blacked out windows and a metal chassis to shield its cargo from...what? The cold? *Or perhaps from prying eyes*, Porter mused.

"I misjudged you," Porter admitted, as he ran a sweaty palm through his matted hair. He realised that JFK had just protected him from his own stupidity, and that the teenage spaceman clearly wasn't planning to murder him. JFK had just saved his life.

But JFK didn't hear Porter's compliment. His mind was in a galaxy far, far away.

"Where did that truck come from?"

Porter swivelled and caught a brief glimpse of the truck's license plate before it vanished into the distance.

He recognised it immediately.

"The truck has come from Lower Denture."

"How do you know?" JFK asked.

"Because," Porter revealed, "I used to live there until my parents took me away."

JFK looked disappointed and he registered his dissatisfaction with a slight frown, the sort of facial expression used by models when advertising swanky new watches.

"The truck is transporting men to work in The Factory," JFK said finally.

"Scabs?" Porter gasped. He instantly thought of Kitty. Should he warn her about this new development in The Strike?

"Those men aren't scabs," JFK said delicately as he walked down the street, nearing his spaceship. "They just want to work. Times are tough, Porter. People are being turned away from food banks. And men with power want everyone fighting to ensure no-one questions their schemes."

Porter suddenly felt very embarrassed.

*

JFK's spaceship was on the outskirts of town, between the school, the hills, and the woods that bisected Castlekrankie. It stood there alone, gleaming in the night, in plain sight.

Porter actually screamed in disbelief when he saw it.

JFK's spaceship wasn't a proper spaceship at all.

It was a garden shed.

A garden shed painted silver.

"You're a loony!" Porter yelled as he bolted in the opposite direction.

"Come back!" JFK cried out. He sounded desperate. "Please come back!"

~~Don't go back to him! He's probably going to slit our throat and drink our blood!~~

"Why don't both of you just bugger off?!"

~~I can't believe you've just disrespected me. Your fate is my fate! We need to work together.~~

"I know who is kidnapping all the teenagers," JFK called out. "Please come back!"

Porter, whose newfound skill at running in Dr Martens was now being put to the test, momentarily paused and shouted back:

"The missing teens are probably locked in your silver shed...without their body parts!"

~~Well that isn't very likely, Porter. I'd wager they're buried on the hills.~~

JFK shouted something back at Porter, but it was indistinguishable with the distance.

Porter was too far away to hear the spaceman.

THE BAD LUCK BIRTHDAY BOY

Porter was regretting his original rash decision to follow the crazy spaceman into the night, but not his decision to flee JFK's silver shed.

He was stranded in the middle of town, forty-five minutes past curfew, and had no idea where he was going. He'd only just become used to going to school in the day; everything looked completely different at night; scary angular buildings, weird lights, street signs that stuck out sharply on lampposts, and 'Missing' posters with teenage faces on them.

"I think I may have overestimated my own intelligence."

Talk about understatement!

"Would you shut up?" Porter told himself. It was getting too hard to concentrate while his other voice ranted inside his brain. His medication was undoubtedly losing power over him; the rainbow's road no longer enough to separate himself from himself.

Calm down and find the nearest road. If you can find a road, then you can safely find a way home. With luck Ma and Pa are too busy hobnobbing with their victims to have returned yet.

"Yeah," Porter said wearily at the night, "they'll be looking for a way to pay for my birthday present."

Porter looked down at his side and studied his nice Dolce & Gabbana leather bag. He felt horrible for accepting it, because when it came to his parents, everything had a price. A birthday gift could never simply a gesture of love; it was always a bribe – an inducement they would reclaim at a later date. Porter didn't want to be at their mercy anymore.

But he also couldn't deny that his new handbag was utterly

fabulous!

~~You are deplorable scum.~~

*

The guilt was always there even when Porter didn't really think about it. It bit gently, at first, whenever it wanted attention. But the more he ignored the guilt, the sharper its teeth became. It was something Porter could never fully escape. He knew it was the price for the years spent helping his parents. Perhaps it had something to do with his brother? Porter didn't think too deeply about the guilt. You don't think about things you're trying to ignore.

But Porter's guilt took on a personality of its own, complete with a noisy, insufferable voice. The voice refused to be silenced! It whispered and hissed and screamed and shouted in Porter's left ear. The medication helped gag the other personality – but it could never completely kill it.

The voice kept him awake at night, saying things – horrible accusatory things.

And Porter agreed with it.

~~You can't smother me inside the squishy bits of your brain!~~
~~I won't be silenced.~~
~~Oh, I just love your new boots!~~
~~Did an old lady pay for them out of her life savings?~~
~~Your parents killed your brother!~~
~~They have to suffer the consequences.~~
~~Once you deal with them…I'll leave you alone.~~
~~I promise.~~

And the voice, it turned out, was a familiar one, from his past.

*

It took him a few minutes of idle wandering, but Porter managed to find a familiar sight on the horizon. The Factory stood out in the distance, black against the night. Porter decided to make his way towards the ugly megastructure. With luck he would find a path that led straight back to Beckham Block. The Factory was now his beacon.

The outlines around him soon made sense, and the paths didn't just lead Porter into cul-de-sacs of no return. The relief that finally, possibly, he knew how to get around Castlekrankie was an energizer and put a little spring in his step.

The streets were eerie. There wasn't a single person out. Not even a dog walker. The curfew had locked the life of Castlekrankie into its homes.

But…Porter stopped…because he realised there *was* someone out, at the end of the street.

He looked around him and quickly realised that he'd wandered into the remains of a little shopping centre. The billboards were garish plastic of different colours. Each shop had a large sign that had been broken off and vandalised with graffiti. EVIL WALKS AMONG US proclaimed one, SCABS OUT warned another. In place of each old shop was a smashed window, hastily patched with splintered wooden panels or rusty metal barricades. The air was thick with the smell of pee and vomit, while discarded bottles of cheap wine rolled idly across the pavements, pushed by the strong night-winds. Porter gagged slightly, and tried breathing through his mouth rather than his nose, because the smell was truly vile. The concrete beneath Porter's expensive boots ~~another damn bribe from your vile parents~~ was encrusted with pigeon shit and flattened chewing gum.

The entire area had been left to die, another casualty of The Strike.

And yet…oddly…there were definitely two people a few metres in front of Porter.

They seemed to be struggling with each other. It looked like a fight of some sort.

"HELLO!" Porter called out. "I'm trying to get to my flat at Beckham Block!"

As a rule, Porter didn't speak to strangers. He felt unnerved by people nearly as much as he felt upset by cracks in the pavement. But it was getting late and Porter was desperate. The last thing he wanted was for his parents to get angry, search his room…and discover his secret mobile telephone. All hell would break loose!

"Are you lost like me?" Porter yelled at the two people.

~~Please don't be a drunk or a drug addict or a murderer!~~

Porter was about to tell himself to shut up when he realised something important.

One of the struggling figures was a teenager, or possibly a child, indistinct but clearly smaller than the taller figure, a man. The teenager's hands were wrapped around the man's throat, as though trying to force him away. It was a violent confrontation. The teenager released the man's throat so he could pull at his legs to try to bring him down. But the taller man violently stamped down at his victim, a frenetic bid to hurt the teenager, or worse. It looked like a murder was being committed.

Porter couldn't see clearly in the gloom, but he did see the man leaning down to punch the smaller figure, who reacted with a frantic flurry of kicks and jabs.

~~Is that man trying to kidnap that kid?~~ the voice in Porter's ear asked uncertainly.

Then the kid fell free onto the pavement. The taller man suddenly broke into a panicked run. He moved quickly towards Porter – far too quickly, his hands outstretched menacingly as he drew closer.

~~He's going to kill us! We're next! And why can't this place afford decent lighting?~~

"Don't worry," Porter babbled. "I won't tell anyone what I've seen…but then I don't know what I've just seen…I mean you might have been trying to give that poor teenager the Heimlich Manoeuvre because he couldn't breathe or...you were strangling him!"

Adrenaline and terror mixed into an intoxicating, unwanted, biological cocktail and made a blithering idiot of Porter Minter.

Porter screamed so loudly that he reached two octaves above Middle C.

Then he turned and ran for his life.

*

Porter reached the same road he had earlier been dragged from by JFK. There was a car in the distance, moving quickly towards him. The twin lights rushed at him but he didn't care. He needed to get away as soon as possible.

"I'm too young to die!" Porter wailed as he frantically waved his arms.

The car came to a sudden halt and the lights flicked off.

Porter exhaled a long chest-lightening sigh of relief at his good fortune, and then he rushed towards his escape vehicle. There was no way a corpse-dragging-killer was going to catch him now! Porter silently applauded himself on his magnificent ingenuity.

The window of the driver's door slid down.

"Thank you," Porter prattled. "I need to get home before my parents discover I'm out!"

A light snapped on inside the car, exposing an unwanted face:

"Happy Birthday," Pa Minter said coldly.

COW FROM MARS

Pain!

Porter gasped as his muscles and joints came back to life. But the sheer pain of being cramped in an enclosed area for hours and hours had taken a toll on him. He tried stretching his arms and legs, and then he pretended to climb a rope so he could pull himself into shape, having heard it improved posture. None of this mattered to Ma or Pa. They stood watching him from the entrance of Beckham Block.

"You'll spend more than just one night sleeping in the back of the car if you ever think of defying us again!" Ma said dispassionately as Porter shook feeling back into his arms. It was too early to get loud, and she couldn't risk waking anyone in the block, lest they should see how she treated her son.

Pa, however, found it difficult to be anything other than rowdy.

"Get inside and get dressed for school."

Porter made for the elevator but Pa stopped him.

"No," he snickered. "You'll use the stairs. You need to lose some weight anyway."

And then he added: "Besides, someone blew up the elevator yesterday with some sort of firework."

Porter found himself grinning as he scaled the stairs to the peak of Beckham Block.

*

Porter made straight for the bathroom, where he soaked himself in extremely hot water. Then he got his clothes out for another day of school. His body moved without direction, because his mind was on holiday, whirring with ideas and plots…a result of all the strange incidents which had taken place within the last few days.

~~You do realise something really obvious don't you?~~

"Yes," Porter replied to himself."

~~The man you saw struggling with his victim probably killed Alfie.~~

Porter didn't say anything aloud, because speaking was unnecessary.

He agreed with his inner voice.

~~And there's something else that you've forgotten about… something from last night.~~

Now this one wasn't obvious to Porter, and he struggled to find an answer.

~~He knows where we live! You told him we were going to Beckham Block!~~

Porter groaned as he remembered that he'd clearly told the mysterious figure in the dark that he was trying to get back to Beckham Block. He had told a killer where he lived! He might as well have yelled his door number and given him keys.

These ominous thoughts were still bothering Porter as entered the living room to get his rucksack for school. He wasn't going to bother watching *Happy Lemontown*; he would just quickly go into the living room and leave again.

That was when he saw the cow.

*

It was a real cow from a real farm.

But it wasn't on a farm…it was in Porter's living room, beside the TV.

"MA! PA! THERE'S A COW IN THE LIVING ROOM!"

"Oh just take your medication, get to school, and stop being so melodramatic," Ma's voice came from the kitchen.

"Moo," the cow said, with a twitch of its nose.

It was a spotty cow, the sort that featured in picture books for toddlers – the sorts of books with bizarre titles like *Cow on a Plough*, *Cows Love Cheese Sandwiches* or *Moo Moo Does A Doo Doo*. And yet the most absurd thing during Porter's week of absurdity was finding a cow in his high-rise home.

Porter crept forward, hoping the cow wouldn't spit on him, ~~do cows actually spit?~~ and carefully extracted his handbag from the wooden chair beside the table. The cow blinked twice at him and Porter found himself patting it gently on the head. Was the cow trying to communicate with him? Perhaps it 'spoke' some sort of special cow language? After that, he headed into the kitchen and gobbled up his acrid rainbow, under the watchful eyes of his parents.

"I'm going to meet my friend Kitty," Porter said quietly.

"Tell her anything about what we do and I'll kill you," Pa said as Porter left.

*

"Come with me!" Kitty said as soon as she laid eyes on Porter.

"Where?" Porter tried to detect if she was concealing any cans of Special Brew about her person. How many cans could someone steal in a day?

"Something amazing has happened to our humble little town!"

Before Porter could protest, or tell her about the cow, he was pulled down the street by the excitable Kitty. She wore her trademark black veil over her eyes, pinned in place by a little black fascinator on her head. Her lips were thick with black lipstick, but she seemed lighter and cheerier than she had been in the graveyard.

Porter didn't resist and allowed her to take him on a fun adventure.

"Where are we going?"

"We aren't going to school, that's for sure!"

Porter waved his handbag menacingly. He hated oblique

answers. Porter wasn't the sort of boy to hit a girl, not even with a well-aimed swipe of an expensive bag, but Kitty sometimes brought out that sentiment in him. He decided not to risk bursting his Dolce & Gabbana with a blow to Kitty's head.

"Yes," Porter said carefully, "I gathered that we aren't going to school from the fact that *we aren't actually going to school.* But where *are* we going?"

Kitty was too excitable to make sense, so didn't bother trying.

She did, however, give away a clue:

"There's a brand new shop in town!"

*

The queues were long, throngs of people animated with anticipation. A new shop promised something special; something none of them had but all of them desperately wanted:

jobs! It would provide work for people now that The Factory no longer did.

"I wonder what the new shop sells."

Porter raised an eyebrow at Kitty's comment, before slyly adding:

"Are you happy that there's a new place for you to steal from?"

Kitty didn't look hurt by his comment, or if she did then Porter couldn't see it for her veil. But her voice trembled slightly when she answered.

"My family would starve if I didn't steal dinner and breakfast for them every day."

And with that she walked away into the crowd.

Porter bit his lip and suddenly felt a stab of remorse at his lack of tact.

But he didn't get long to wallow in self-pity.

A sleek limousine parted the crowds and slowly, deliberately, came to a halt at the entrance of the new shop. Porter craned his neck in the direction of the shop windows, because he finally had an opportunity to see what this new shop sold.

The windows were crammed with food – in tins, cartons, and packets.

Porter shivered when his eyes fell on a tub of powdered custard.

The entrance to the shop was open but protected by a lovely yellow ribbon.

~~There must be a famous star in the limousine!~~

"That is logical," Porter muttered to himself.

~~I bet whoever they've got to open the new shop will cut that ribbon!~~

"I wish they'd cut your throat!"

~~Ah but my throat is your throat! Do you understand the concept of symbiosis?~~

"Damn!" Porter muttered, soundly trounced by his other personality.

And that's the moment the door of the limousine swung open to reveal…

~~I'm wrong. It isn't a famous star.~~

Porter felt sick with revulsion and loathing. It wasn't an exaggeration to say he felt as though he'd been contaminated by a dirty bomb of grimy grossness, or something you stand on but can't clean off.

It was Miss Happy Lemon Washington.

She wore a simple suit of lemon, with a pair of Jackie Onassis sunglasses, also lemon. Her hair had a frosting of yellow glitter, giving it a glowing, sparkly aura that exploded with light whenever a blast from the clicking cameras hit it. Her lips were curled into her trademark smile, but Porter shuddered at the sight of it, because he had witnessed a smile like that during his time flicking through TV channels to find National Geographic. It had been a show about killer piranha fish, which ripped other fish to pieces with their sharp teeth, smiling whilst they worked, happy little murderers.

Porter wanted to scream, but the sound would only come out as a snarl. The sound a person makes when they're throwing up. He couldn't help it! Miss Happy Lemon Washington was even more terrifying than the man Porter had caught fighting the teenage boy the previous night.

Kitty appeared by Porter's side, her fit of pique seemingly over. They stood united, their friendship bolstered by their simmering hate of Happy Washington.

"She would turn up to the opening of a cereal box!" Porter jeered.

"But is she a serial killer?" Kitty asked innocently.

They laughed and any insult Porter had dealt Kitty was suddenly forgotten.

Miss Happy Lemon Washington sashayed past them, her bodyguards pushing their way to the front of the crowd with a subtle air of violence. Porter caught a whiff of her overpowering perfume, a monstrous assault upon his nostrils. But if her adoring public objected to being pushed around, or suffocated, they didn't show it.

Instead they cheered and hollered delightedly for their local Queen Of All Television, a title which, incidentally, Miss Happy Lemon Washington bestowed upon herself.

*

It didn't take long for Porter to realise he was wrong.

Miss Happy Lemon Washington wasn't there to cut the ribbon for a new shop.

She was there to cut the ribbon to open a **food bank**.

But there was more.

Something extraordinary happened, though no-one really noticed it other than Porter. Something downright weird that most people *wouldn't* notice. Especially if they were star-struck in the presence of a Z-list television presenter.

Miss Happy Lemon Washington stood chatting for five minutes.

And not once did she blink.

Not. Once.

Only Porter knew what this truly meant. He knew the signs right away.

"SHE'S AN ALIEN!"

~~AND WE HAVE TO KILL HER BEFORE SHE EATS OUR BRAINS!~~

"What?"

"Who are you talking to?" Kitty asked.

Kitty looked utterly befuddled, and Porter quickly realised that she was beginning to question his mental stability. ~~Well it's about time someone did!~~ Porter literally talked to himself. He needed to try and remember to do it when people couldn't see him in conversation. The fact that he had a dazzling collection of handbags and sympathy for scabs probably wouldn't do his social standing any good either.

Porter smiled his version of a vibrant smile (as vibrant as tea-stained teeth can be vibrant) and Kitty quickly forgot the weirdness she'd witnessed.

Instead, she asked a question:

"What happened to your scab friend?"

Porter didn't have a clue what she was talking about.

"My scab friend?"

"You walked to school with him on your first day."

"Alfie!"

"Yes, the scab boy. What happened to him?"

But Porter couldn't reply.

He didn't know the answer to her question.

SPACED INVADERS

Porter Minter kneeled on the floor at the edge of his bed and prayed to God.

"I don't know what to do," he said as he looked up at the religious iconography on his bedroom wall. Kindly eyes looked down at him, never blinking, but ever wise. This was an emergency, and Porter needed all the assistance he could get from this divine figure.

"When I lack direction in life, I know your wisdom will guide me. I always ask myself…what would *you* do? You are omnipotent and perfect. I know you can help me."

Porter opened his eyes and looked up at his all-powerful God.

It was David Tennant, the tenth Doctor Who.

"I am weak and human, but you are more than human and will surely give me the advice I crave! You see, I think I know who's kidnapping everyone in town. She's a force of pure evil, though she smiles constantly. Always grinning like a psychopath."

The poster didn't look convinced.

Porter backtracked slightly, attempting to explain why he was determined in his quest.

"Alfie is my friend…well, he isn't really my friend…I don't really know him, if I'm being honest. But he was there when I needed a friend. That car is a horrible jail and he rescued me from it. So you see, oh mighty one, I need to repay the debt."

David Tennant said nothing.

Because he was a poster pinned on a wall.

Porter started to get a little bit irritated with his idol.

"You're a tough audience," Porter admonished the poster.

But it said nothing, preferring to stay in an action pose with Catherine Tate.

"Do you think I should track down JFK and get him to explain everything to me?"

The poster didn't reply, but Porter took this as a good sign.

"Yes, that's what I'll do."

*

~~And you say I'm crazy!~~ a little voice in the back of Porter's left ear whispered as he fled Beckham Block and ventured out onto the fractured pavements and weird streets of Castlekrankie with his handbag straps wrapped around his left arm.

Yes, Porter said without speaking, *we're both a little bit crazy.*

*

Porter had never played truant in his life, but Kitty had introduced him to the concept and suddenly he felt free: completely, magnificently, utterly liberated from structure and routine and boring lessons! Kitty was at school, but they were going to meet after lessons ended. She wasn't quite ready to stay off the entire day; and with all the missing names on the register, she was worried the teachers would think she too had been abducted.

But Porter was under no such obligation.

There were other schools in other towns.

And he would be sent to them once his parents were finished in Castlekrankie.

*

The shed that was supposed to be JFK's spaceship looked less silver in the daylight and more sulphur grey, making it seem even cheaper than by the light of the silver-bestowing Moon. It wasn't too far from the gates of Castlekrankie High School and seemed to have been a bicycle shed in a past life.

Porter took a deep breath.

Then he knocked four times on the wooden door of JFK's 'spaceship'.

There was no reply.

Porter reached out, gently pushed the door, and let himself in...

*

The inside of the shed was in complete disarray. It looked as if someone had smashed everything to pieces. An old computer, with the Castlekrankie High School logo stuck onto the base, had been pummelled so violently that it chilled Porter slightly. Someone really had unleashed a suppressed fury on the inside of JFK's spaceship.

~~It can't have been JFK. He wasn't the man we saw struggling with that teenager last night.~~

"Who says it was a man we saw last night?" Porter cautioned himself against jumping to hasty conclusions. "It could easily be a woman who's stealing people from the streets of Castlekrankie. A big, tall, man-shaped woman!"

~~Ah! Are you still obsessing over your Miss Happy Lemon Washington theory?~~

"She didn't blink once this morning at the food bank!"

Porter bent over to pick up the remains of a weird tricorder scanning device. ~~That's an outdated iPod with a wire aerial glued onto the top!~~ It was a ridiculous looking contraption.

~~By the way, Porter, there's something else you should know.~~

"What?"

~~There's someone standing right behind us!~~

Porter cautiously turned around to see someone holding a nasty-looking gun.

It was aimed at Porter's head.

MEMORANDUM

to:	Sir Hemmingford Higginson
from:	Sergeant Major Darryl Jones
subject:	GENERAL HENDERSON HAS GONE MISSING!

The General has gone missing. We're concerned because the local press was reporting a lot of sudden disappearances with no explanation. Now The Professor has gone missing too.

We have conducted a search and turned up nothing.

I have posted two men outside the Infirmary but it isn't a popular job. The men don't want to go near the Infirmary. Some of them claim to have heard screams in the middle of the night, but the only people inside the Infirmary are the sleepers. One of my most reliable men told me personally that he had heard someone in the Infirmary *giggling*, but again when we checked we found no-one.

We require assistance.

JFK EXPLAINS IT ALL

"Are you an agent of the Supreme Overlord of All Evil?" JFK asked.

"Is the Supreme Overlord of All Evil actually Miss Happy Lemon Washington?"

JFK, still clad in his white spacesuit, lowered the homemade ray gun slowly. He seemed puzzled, his face framed with confusion and just a tad of suspicion. Porter couldn't believe the teenage astronaut would possibly think him capable of breaking into his spaceship and smashing it to pieces. All those broken cracked things! Porter shuddered.

No, someone else had wrecked his home.

"I swear I didn't do it!" Porter cried out, purely to convince JFK of his trustworthiness

"I don't think you did this," JFK said blandly. He lowered the gun and looked around the interior of his homemade spaceship. "The Supreme Overlord of All Evil has been here," he cried out excitedly.

Porter didn't know what was happening, he needed some of it explained to him, but he couldn't deny the thrill of excitement he was feeling.

"The Alien From Another Dimension?"

"Yes."

JFK suddenly burst into a flurry of motion, desperately ransacking the mess to see if the intruder had taken something from him. He relaxed when he realised there was nothing missing.

"I want you to tell me everything that's going on," Porter demanded, trying his best to maintain a sort of composure.

"You won't run away this time?"

~~That was below the belt!~~

"No. I want the truth."

JFK looked about for a chair, which he found tilted upside down at the far side of the ship. He offered it to Porter, who took it so he could rest his weary ankles. He asked for a separate chair for his handbag, because Porter always had a seat especially for his expensive bags, but JFK only had two chairs and one of them was for himself.

JFK eased himself onto a chair and told Porter a story he swore was absolutely true.

His story was filled with aliens, spaceships, and violent, bloody war.

*

"Once upon a time," JFK began.

~~No! No! No! You don't start off a story with Once Upon A Time. That is a terrible cliché and I am too much of a cliché-crusher to sit inside your head without protesting!~~

"Shut up," Porter hissed loudly.

"I thought you wanted to know why everyone in town is going missing."

"Sorry," Porter reddened, "I didn't mean you!"

JFK continued with a slight frown on his model face.

~~You might as well start a story with a long and boring description about how you woke up in the morning and had your breakfast and...~~

Porter blocked out his other voice as it ranted about narrative technique. It was difficult, but he found JFK's tone – a serious voice with a slight American accent – more relaxing and eventually it supplanted the other voice.

The story, however, was utterly unbelievable.

"It was when the alien fleet attacked us at Omicron Beta that it all went wrong…"

*

JFK, the youngest of the three survivors, blinked wearily as he read the latest war reports on the holosphere in front of him. Data glimmered before his face in the form of casualty numbers, photographs, news and obituaries. He was tired from a day of combat and the stimulants, which were fed through his suit into a small puncture on his neck, were losing their potency. He couldn't sleep. He wanted to sleep more than anything, but he couldn't do it anymore.

"War is hell," said his co-pilot, a man in his thirties whose surname was Winston. He sported a tired smile.

"So is insomnia," JFK replied quickly.

Winston and JFK waited for the third pilot to say something, but he remained slumped and silent on the bed behind them. The escape capsule was cramped and even though it had a bed for each soldier, none of them used theirs.

How could they use a bed when they couldn't sleep?

"Do you think the fleet will win?"

JFK didn't know how to answer Winston. He barely knew his other pilots, but they were the only survivors from their ship, so he knew the men were trustworthy.

The third pilot groaned in pain, his body assailed by hidden agonies.

At first JFK thought he was having a bad dream, but that couldn't be.

For him to have a bad dream, he would need to be asleep.

And sleep was impossible for all of them.

That was when the third pilot opened his eyes.

"He's awake," Winston said with noticeable relief.

But JFK saw the eyes and realised something was horribly wrong.

The third pilot blinked bright green, his smile wide and spiteful.

JFK swiftly raised his pistol and fired at the third pilot's head. It burst open, spraying cherry-coloured brain rain across the core of the ship. Winston yelled in fear and panic. As a soldier, he knew exactly what was happening.

"The Alien took over his body!" JFK cried as the capsule swerved through a cloud of space debris, the remains of ships caught up in the war, or victims of the meteor belt.

Winston pulled the control lever of the capsule towards him until it stuck.

"The meteor bombardment is getting tougher to navigate!"

"I didn't know his name," JFK said of the unfortunate third pilot.

"His name was Martin," Winston said flatly.

He looked up at JFK with eyes full of sadness.

And when he blinked, he blinked vivid blazing green.

JFK went for his pistol.

Winston was too fast! He grabbed JFK by his wrist and twisted viciously. JFK tugged until he was free of Winston – or the thing that now inhabited his body – and then fell back, back, back until he slammed down hard onto the slick floor of the escape capsule.

JFK looked up to see Winston stepping over the pilot chair, moving slowly towards him. The creature piloting the pilot was trying to work his weak human body. This was typical of the thing they were battling; a monster with the power to take possession of human beings, hitchhiking through them until it found the perfect home to stay in forever.

You stupid little child! Winston hissed in the voice of The Alien. *You really think you can stand against me? You are a sack of meat and bone and blood! You are mine to command…and destroy.*

JFK tried desperately to reach his gun, which was holstered on his hip, but the hand he usually drew with seared in excruciating pain. There was a possibility that it was dislocated. JFK moved his free hand around his waist to locate his holster.

Winston's eyes flared with hot sickly-green light.

I am The Alien From Another Dimension. Your world screams out for my domination! And if you get in my way...I will sweep you and your insignificant species aside!

Winston threw himself down at JFK with clawed hands.

JFK grabbed his gun and fired.

It was a bad shot, missing the head completely.

But it punched a hole in Winston's ribcage, so it wasn't all bad.

The co-pilot fell dead onto the floor.

JFK lay there, breathing hard, relieved to be alive and himself.

But without his co-pilots, he couldn't steer his ship properly.

He wasn't surprised when his escape capsule crash-landed on Earth.

*

Not only did he crash-land on Earth, but he somehow ended up in a town named Castlekrankie, which looked even more desolate than Mars.

"Damn," he said as he surveyed his new surroundings.

He breathed in the fresh air, a sweet tang he couldn't get enough of after months breathing recycled oxygen. But the air was mixed with something else...a spicy scent.

JFK wandered through the strange town until he tracked down the source of the beautiful pepperiness that was setting his nostrils alight.

"What in the seven galaxies is that amazing smell?"

It wasn't long until he found the answer to this question.

It came in the form of a sign hanging outside a shop:

KWIK KEBAB: <u>We do Kebabs, Chips, Wraps and Marlowe Meat Pies!</u>

*

The staff of the Castlekrankie branch of 'Kwik Kebab' couldn't believe their eyes when a spaceman walked through the door and asked for takeaway. He had no money, but he did have a funny-looking gun, so they gave him what he wanted, just to make him leave.

*

JFK was bored. He had spent weeks trying to find ways of repairing the ship's damaged systems, but they weren't compatible with primitive Earth technology. "You'd better work," he told the holosphere as he tinkered around with it. The screwdriver in his hand wasn't a good replacement for a sonic lance, but it did the job.

Suddenly, delightfully, the sphere came to life and JFK finally had TV.

Four hundred channels, absolutely free!

He surfed through all his new channels until he found the local news station.

The words of a journalist caught his ear and chilled him:

Three teenagers have disappeared without trace. Local authorities are baffled by this recent spate of disappearances. In other news, union negotiations at The Factory appear to have broken down...

JFK knew from watching the news that The Alien was now at work in Castlekrankie.

"It escaped from the shuttle!" JFK yelled angrily at himself.

But where was it? And more importantly...*who* was it?

*

"So what you're saying is that The Alien is stealing people for their bodies?"

"Yes," JFK replied flatly.

"And this Alien From Another Dimension could be anyone?"

Even saying the words aloud terrified Porter, because he

understood better than anyone what it was to hear voices that no-one else could hear. But he didn't want to alarm his strange new friend.

Nor did he want to make him think he was responsible for killing the missing teenagers.

"That's how it survives," JFK explained grimly. "It stays inside a host victim and strikes when it feels threatened. The host might not be aware that they're hosting The Alien."

~~It isn't me!~~

Porter stood up, rubbed down his black velvet trousers with both hands because he felt grubby sitting on the chair JFK had provided, and then made an important announcement:

"What you've just described isn't alien infiltration. It's a medical condition called Schizophrenia. Maybe the killer is schizophrenic, in which case he or she needs help."

JFK stood up and faced Porter, his eyes wide with the sort of realisation that only comes when all the pieces are in place.

"How do you know?" he asked guardedly.

~~Tell him the truth!~~

Porter sighed.

"I know because…well…I just know…."

JFK backed away slowly, not wanting to accept what he was being told.

"I'm technically, medically, socially and awkwardly schizophrenic," Porter prattled, conscious of the fact he probably looked like a psychopath.

JFK looked around wildly for his ray gun as Porter tried frantically to convince the teenage spaceman that he wasn't a threat.

"I'm a loony and I hate cracks in the pavement, unsolved mysteries, awful children's TV presenters, and ugly handbags."

His words were being soundly ignored.

"But I'm *not* a serial killer!"

JFK slowly raised his ray gun until it was level with Porter.

Porter's life flashed before his eyes in the form of a rubbish newspaper headline:

SPACED OUT BOY MURDERED BY SPACEMAN!
Teenager With Expensive And Absolutely Genuine Dolce & Gabbana Bag Found Dead. At Least He Looked Trendy.

Porter closed his eyes as the sound of screaming forced him to block his mouth with a clenched fist.

But the screaming didn't stop.

It was only when Porter removed his hand from his mouth that he realised the obvious.

The scream was coming from outside the shed.

It belonged to a girl!

IT'S THE END OF THE WORLD
AS WE KNOW IT

Sissy McNamee watched as each teenager passed through the doors of the canteen, looking for the lunch that would ultimately be the only meal of the day for many of them. But as hungry as Sissy felt, and as weak as her grip on the sign was, she would neither break nor bend nor yield before the tyrannical headmaster and his murderous policies.

Every time someone looked over at Sissy, she waved her sign harder, to highlight the slogan and give it the power it deserved. Not many looked at her. But Sissy refused to blend into the background. She was fighting a war against her disgusting classmates.

"Eat a burger," someone yelled boisterously at the far end of the canteen.

Another voice jeered: "Attention whore!"

"You're as bad as the scabs!" Sissy screamed back at them, her voice boosted by indignation. How could they ignore her? How could they laugh at her message?

There was only one phrase on her placard, a battle cry lovingly painted during art class:

MILK IS COW RAPE!

*

Sissy decided to take the fight away from school and head over to the most evil place in Castlekrankie. It was worse than The Steak Place, McDonalds and KFC. In Sissy's opinion it was even worse than The Factory. It was a place of pure wickedness.

It was the local farm, a place she knew very well.

Sissy moved her signs and headed off. Her hair, the colour of roses, was curly and wild – a result of Sissy refusing to use hair product to tame her curls, because most hair products were tested on animals. She couldn't bear the idea of innocent little rabbits being forced to wear makeup meant for bimbos!

It took twenty minutes on the X39 to reach the farm.

Sissy felt her perpetual sense of outrage return as the farm came into view, obscured by dirty windows but within reach of the bus.

She got out and headed to the main townhouse.

Sissy was going to do a little bit of spying.

*

The townhouse was an old building with patches of modern embellishment. Strong old sandstone bricks with white plastic double-glazed windows spliced into them. The roof of the townhouse was made up of old slates sitting uncomfortably with nice new ones. And the conservatory looked completely at odds with the rest of the farm, the new architecture making an odd coupling alongside the bales of hay sitting by the car park.

The Factory was all but dead.

The Farm, however, still teemed with life.

But Sissy knew that an ethical life could never be lived under these unethical conditions.

*

She crept up to the front door of the townhouse, avoiding the enemy by the chicken coop. Sissy saw and felt the heat of the red mist whilst watching as Farmer Derek, the owner of everything around her, pushed a chicken back through the same cage door she had opened earlier that day. The damn farmer was locking them up again.

Sissy was so engrossed in watching the farmer that she

failed to notice someone creeping up behind her. It wasn't until a dainty hand reached out to gently touch her shoulder that she realised she had been caught!

Sissy whirled around to see a woman looking down at her, a middle-aged wife with thick curly red hair and a pink velour tracksuit. There was concern in her eyes and unease in her voice as she said:

"What on earth are you doing with those signs?"

"Hello, Mum," Sissy said rebelliously.

"Your dad has been out here all morning trying to get the hens back in their cages." Her voice lowered conspiratorially, "Someone opened the cage doors. Was it you?"

"YES!" Sissy yelled, attracting the attention of her father over at the coop.

"And one of our cows has gone missing…Sissy dear, was that you too?"

"YES!" she lied.

Then she turned and ran away, with her signs still stuck to her back.

Sissy knew her father wouldn't be angry. He was too busy exploiting the animals in the farm to notice her distress. He cared about the farm more than he would ever care about her. She could never get him to treat her like his daughter.

So she ran as fast as she could.

She would never return home.

*

When Sissy got back into town it was still bright – bright but cold – and she was confident in the knowledge that the curfew wasn't for another few hours. She would be safe, but maybe the curfew would freak out her parents. That could be her ultimate weapon!

Sissy smiled at the thought of her hysterically worried parents, hugging her and begging her not to run away ever again. They would do anything! They would give her the car she wanted for her birthday; yes, even the car! They would set the hens free. And they would never ever use milk in their tea.

"Milk is cow rape," Sissy said to a motley crew of men, strikers from The Factory who were on their way back to the picket line. The strikers gave her odd looks and quickened their pace to get away.

Sissy stood alone with her placard by the side of the road, looking around at the empty streets. Then she decided to head back to school. There was still time for her to stand outside the main entrance with her placards. That would get her some attention!

Sissy was close to Castlekrankie High when she suddenly felt…a presence…nearby.

She stopped and turned. But no-one was following her.

Sissy shook her head wryly and continued towards school.

*

She didn't have a chance to turn again.

Something long and thin and sharp pricked her arm.

She screamed in surprise as she was pulled away from the school gates. She tried to kick and punch at her attacker, but it gained her nothing. Her terrified screams were so loud that even Porter and JFK heard them from The Spaceship At The End Of The Street.

By the time they'd followed the sound of screams to the place where Sissy had been caught, she was already gone. The lights had taken her far away.

The only remaining signs of Sissy were her plywood signs.

They had been violently snapped in half.

HANDBAG OF HATE!

The mere fact that someone had been taken in broad daylight didn't even make the local news. Porter supposed that so many teenagers had vanished in Castlekrankie that it had simply stopped being news and instead had become... commonplace, even expected.

Instead the big breaking news story was something very odd indeed:

The remains of a cow had been found on the hills.

They had been positioned in the centre of the crop circle, of course.

*

Porter turned the TV off and waited for Ma and Pa to get out of their bed. They had obviously been out late again, if what he'd just caught on the news was true. Sitting alone in the living room was nice, though a bit uncomfortable because it reeked of cow shit. He had plenty of time to kill before he needed to head off to school. And Porter was determined to confront his parents. Enough was enough. It was now or never. Things *had* to be said, questions *had* to be asked, if only to release the build-up of tension in his brain. His skull felt close to breaking point.

His parents announced their presence with noises including flushing toilets, petty bickering, the kettle being boiled and a microwave being put to good use for – of all things – a breakfast of chicken tikka masala.

"As if our flat doesn't smell bad enough!" Porter griped as his hand tightened around the straps of his Dolce & Gabbana. He could feel a funny mood coming on, and when that happened...people usually got smacked around by a flying handbag.

Ma was the first to notice Porter sitting quietly by the main dining table.

"Have you taken your medication?"

"Hello, Son," Porter said sarcastically, "how are you doing this morning? I hope you're having a good time in your new home. How was school? I know I haven't asked, Son, but that's because *I'm too busy kidnapping cows to notice!*"

Ma didn't flinch one bit.

Pa sauntered into the room. His tatty pink bathrobe (which had been red when he'd first bought it) already had some curry stains on it. The microwave clearly hated him too. Porter wondered what would happen if the microwave talked like the elevator.

"You stole that cow and you killed it."

Ma and Pa didn't even attempt to lie.

"Yes," Pa said with a shrug. He stabbed a piece of curried chicken and chewed it.

"Why?" Porter felt quietly depressed for the poor cow.

"Because we want the people of this godforsaken town to think aliens are trying to communicate with them. And everyone knows aliens dismember cows."

Pa seemed extremely proud of his warped logic.

Porter asked a question, his voice steady, flat and controlled:

"Do you have anything to do with the disappearing teenagers?"

Ma and Pa looked away from their son. And burst into cackles of co-ordinated laughter.

"What's so funny about teenagers being murdered?" Porter yelled above the noise.

"I don't care about dead brats," Ma said calmly. "These people are nothing but walking wallets. They are here to be exploited, do you understand?"

Porter felt his lungs contract and suddenly he was unsteady on his feet

"You have no compassion for anyone other than yourselves. You murdered my brother!"

The laughter immediately stopped.

Violence started as quickly as the laughter had ended.

Pa leaped over the couch and swung for Porter.

Porter ducked skilfully and, with a rising curve, turned his handbag into an extension of his fist, delivering a mighty uppercut. His father shot across the living room until he crashed into the dining table, which helped break his awkward fall. Porter had prepared for this eventuality, and unzipped his handbag to reveal the secret of its power.

Cans of custard, tightly packed.

Porter had turned his birthday handbag into the ultimate weapon.

"UNGRATEFUL BRAT!" Ma screamed as she threw herself at her son, hands outstretched, her fake nails more than a match for Porter's custard-can-powered Dolce & Gabbana bag.

~~Proceed with caution!~~ The other voice sounded terrified. ~~This one is a psycho!~~

Porter ignored the whispering voice in his left ear and let his instincts guide him. He stood poised with both hands on his handbag, ready to bring it down over Ma's head, but there was a slight problem.

Well, not a problem, more a major miscalculation.

The bottom of the handbag burst, releasing the cans of custard onto the carpet and causing even more chaos.

And that's when Porter noticed something else genuinely awful about his handbag.

"THIS ISN'T A REAL DOLCE & GABBANA!!!"

Instinct no longer guided Porter in his retribution; instead he allowed rage to conquer him. He threw the tattered remains of his fake Dolce & Gabbana at Ma. Then he kicked the remaining cans of custard at her with skilful punts that he couldn't even have replicated on a football field. Each kick propelled each can through the air; compact, hard projectiles with a gloopy aftershock. It was the least his parents deserved after giving him a fake handbag. *Goodness*, Porter thought angrily, *the stitching is too unsteady to be the work of the real Dolce & Gabbana! How could I not have noticed it?* ~~Yes how could you not have noticed it? The shame of it! We've been toting fake goods. This is a dark day for us.~~

"Please stop it!" Pa yelled tearfully. He was in agony from the fall he'd suffered.

"Please don't kill us!" Ma pleaded with wide, naive eyes.

"Then tell me the truth!"

Ma retreated and bent over to help her husband to his feet. They both seemed genuinely shaken after being assaulted by their handbag-wielding offspring. Ma didn't break eye contact with her son the entire time.

"Why do you think we're responsible for kidnapping the missing teenagers?" Pa asked.

"You have previous history when it comes to people disappearing," Porter replied, deliberately glancing out into the hallway cupboard where his brother resided in a suitcase. He wanted them to know that he knew his brother hadn't been abducted by aliens as a child. They'd killed him. And it was time they talked about it.

Pa's voice suddenly turned nasty. "You think *we* killed your brother?"

"We knew about the teenagers," Ma revealed in a shaky voice, "and we knew that Castlekrankie has a reputation for being the country's biggest UFO hotspot. It made sense for us to move here and take advantage of the situation. After all, didn't our son – your brother – vanish after seeing a UFO?"

The way she said it chilled Porter to the very core of his

being. The sheer casualness of his mother talking about conning people out of their money when they were deep in grief. She was a loony, and quite dangerous. But at least she was openly talking about her other son, Porter's late brother.

Porter took a little comfort in that, for reasons he couldn't understand.

"Did your stupid little press conference convince people to ask you for help?"

"Yes! Not everyone believes that we can talk to aliens, of course, but it only takes one or two people with life savings to give us what we want!" Ma said this enthusiastically, warming to the subject at hand. Pa didn't speak. He was content to let his wife talk for him.

"Ma, what you're doing is wrong on so many levels. These teenagers – some of them in my classes at school – they aren't being abducted by an alien. I think someone is killing them. Both of you have to stop this at once! You're helping a crazy cretin cover up his tracks. The crop circles, the dead cow, the press conference. It confuses everything."

Pa snickered, a horrible little noise, and then covered his mouth.

"What are you laughing at?"

"You're right, Son. Aliens didn't abduct your big brother."

"He was murdered," Ma admitted sadly, a tear dripping down her face.

"But *we* didn't murder him!" Pa said quickly.

"Then who was it? Because he didn't get into that suitcase by himself."

*

Ma and Pa couldn't stop laughing.

Porter wasn't prepared for what they said next:

"It was you, Porter. *You* killed him."

What? But I'm not dead. I'm here, inside your head!

PRINCESS JASMINE OF PLANET POUND

Kitty was bored at school and not for the first time that day did her thoughts turn to the curious new boy in her life. Porter, she decided, was completely unreadable. She just couldn't work him out at all. She hadn't seen him since they'd parted ways outside the food bank. He hadn't come to school. Few people came to school these days.

And the ones who made it didn't last very long.

Kitty looked around at the spaces in the chairs where her classmates had once sat.

"They're all missing?" she asked incredulously, whilst lifting up her black veil just in case she couldn't see everyone. No, there was nothing wrong with her eyesight.

English Class Period Five was virtually abandoned.

"Not ALL of them," Miss Gorham declared with the odd inflections in her voice. "Cameron Whyte's mother PHONED in for HIM today. He HASN'T left the TOILET since LAST night, and though I'd feel bad for him, he IS the son of a SCAB."

Kitty stood up, raised her head high, raised her first even further, and declared:

"It's a government conspiracy!"

Miss Gorham chuckled gently.

"Please tell ME who is in CHARGE of this CONSPIRACY? Don't tell ME you BELIEVE all that NONSENSE in the NEWSPAPERS about ALIENS in Castlekrankie? It's RUBBISH! Those two LOONIES from Lower Denture need locked up! There are NO aliens, NO spaceships, NO government conspiracies...and there is NO murderer lurking in the bushes at night in Castlekrankie."

Miss Gorham was absolutely right about Ma and Pa Minter.

She was also quite right to point out that the newspapers were printing rubbish.

But she was absolutely wrong about everything else.

*

Kitty left Mrs Gorham's class with a disquieting sensation of worry; not the usual worry of starvation and rent arrears, but something else…something different. She didn't know what it was until she passed the wall of MISSING posters.

More posters had been added. Many faces that looked down at her were old friends and classmates, some of whom no longer came to school. They probably never would come to school ever again.

"Why would the government kidnap innocent teenagers?"

The truth was out there; or so Kitty thought as she moved slowly across corridors, down stairwells, until she reached her final class of the day – in this case, History.

Ideas – crazy ideas – and thoughts were playing leapfrog in Kitty's brain.

"There has to be a pattern to the disappearances!"

Kitty found herself bypassing History. *Who cares about history when there's no future?* she thought bitterly. *No-one cares about us anymore. They're all obsessed with the strike and fighting each other.*

"And the violence has suddenly become worse in recent months," she mused aloud.

A few minutes passed before Kitty realised she had bypassed the school gates as well as History.

She was off to do her favourite kind of shopping: the five-fingered-discount kind!

*

Kitty sauntered through the remains of the dodgem cars –

once vibrantly painted carriages of fun that were now rotted and disused, unloved and abandoned. The remnants of the once proud Joy Land held a particular allure for Kitty, who had spent many a day on the rides between eating the fluffy pink candy floss and stealing coconuts from the coconut stalls.

"This is why I go to work," her dad used to tell her as they soared up high on the Twisted Terror Trial roller coaster. It would shoot up...and then crash down.

"Just like my life," Kitty said aloud as metal creaked in the breeze.

She moved away from the rides of Joy Land, eventually finding her way to the outskirts of The Factory. Kitty was so close she could see signs pointing towards the enormous iron gates that thousands used to pass through every day, her father included. Kitty saw a group of men in tattered jeans and scruffy jackets, all standing together clutching signs that said EQUAL PAY FOR ALL.

They were sharing coins, attempting to scrape together enough money to pay for a Marlowe Meat Pie for lunch.

Kitty felt a kind of spiritual pain at the injustice of the situation.

What is one pie divided between *eight* men?

*

Stanley Jackson, the new security guard at the Castlekrankie branch of Planet Pound, and a supporter of The Strike, watched as Kitty methodically stole bits and pieces from every shelf she visited. She was an oddball, a girl who always dressed like she was attending the Salem Witch Trials. But she made Stanley smile inside. Her hats were large, her black veil never moved away from her eyes, which he knew were constantly tearstained: but most importantly, her gloved hands were magnets for everything.

He never allowed the smile to reach his face. CCTV might catch it and the people in the office would know he was turning a blind eye to the girl's rampant thievery. Stan couldn't help it. He knew the strikers were in absolute poverty.

He knew because he had worked in The Factory.

So he simply stood aside, pretending to find another customer utterly fascinating.

What Stan didn't know was that someone else was watching the girl.

And it was another girl.

*

Kitty was about to steal a brand new ironing board when a horsey voice froze her to the spot.

"Katherine Stomp! What are you doing here? Does your daddy know you're a thief?"

Then there was a premeditated pause from the other voice, before it added something else to the verbal ambush – and it was devastating in its viciousness.

"Oh, I forgot. Your daddy is *dead*."

Kitty gently returned the ironing board to the shelf she had snatched it from. She took a few deep breaths, because she wanted to be calm when she confronted the hateful owner of the horsey voice. She then turned and showed only a smile, for her eyes remained hidden behind her funeral veil.

"Princess Jasmine of Planet Pound," Kitty snarled.

*

Princess Jasmine of Planet Pound wasn't a real princess, though if you asked her she would probably tell you otherwise. She felt like a princess, and she acted like one. She was a graceful girl with poise and pretention…and a sneering upturned mouth that looked like a frown even when she smiled. But she lacked the supposed good breeding of actual royalty. An unpleasant child from the moment she'd slipped out of her mother's womb, Princess Jasmine wanted for nothing but desired everything.

Her father, the owner of Planet Pound, lavished his princess with her heart's desire.

This was ironic because everyone at school knew Princess Jasmine didn't have a heart.

*

"Were you trying to steal an ironing board? I bet you've stuffed your clothes with food too! Well...food and paper tissues, if you get my meaning!"

Princess Jasmine of Planet Pound stood with her hands on her hips. She was dressed in pink, a lovely expensive dress funded from the hard work of underpaid staff. It looked like something Alice would wear in Wonderland to a wonderfully mad tea party, but Princess Jasmine was more Malice in Blunderland than Alice in Wonderland.

Kitty said nothing. She knew it was futile. She had been caught red-handed.

"Are you a thief?" Princess Jasmine yelled loudly in a bid to embarrass Kitty in public.

And it worked, for the sparse few customers in the shop stopped to watch the fun.

"It depends," Kitty shot back, "on whether or not *you're* my psychotherapist?"

*

A few minutes later and Kitty was escorted out of Planet Pound by a policeman. As she looked back, she heard Princess Jasmine screaming at the old security guard by the door. Kitty hadn't realised he'd known she was stealing from the store. She wanted to rush back and hug the old man, but she was already in the police car.

And the security guard was no longer a security guard.

The brat had taken his job off him, in another public shaming.

*

The police car stopped halfway down the street, much to Kitty's surprise.

She lifted her veil to see a familiar face peering back at her:

"Hello," Officer Robert Hatfield said with a slightly jagged smile.

"You were at my school!" Kitty exclaimed.

"Yes, I was," he said warmly, "and now I'm letting you go."

Then, as she left the car, he raised a fist and added:

"I believe in The Strike."

And he drove away, leaving an astonished Kitty marvelling at her good luck.

But her luck would soon run out.

MEMORANDUM

to:	Sergeant Major Darryl Jones
from:	Sir Hemmingford Higginson
subject:	GENERAL HENDERSON HAS GONE MISSING!

I will send a task force to Castlekrankie.
We will find The Professor.
We will take charge of everything.

SPACEBOY SUPERMODEL
OF THE UNIVERSE

Porter came to Kitty's house later that same evening.

"Does anyone care about the curfew?" Kitty asked with a trace of derision in her voice.

"Not since the mothership landed," Porter replied.

"Why are you here, Porter?"

The crisp night air bit into Kitty's skin, but it wasn't the cold that took her breath away. It was what happened next, because she couldn't believe what Porter said:

"I need you to steal something for me."

Kitty opened her mouth to say NO when she caught a glimpse of Porter's friend.

He moved into view, appearing through the black gossamer material of her veil, and though he'd been there with Porter all along....Kitty finally *saw* him for the first time.

A teenage boy dressed-up like a spaceman, complete with space helmet and some sort of weird ray gun holstered at his hip.

The boy smiled shyly at Kitty. He looked like someone from a boyband, a face straight out of the pages of WE LOVE POP.

"I'll come out with you," she said immediately.

*

They walked together down the street, away from the houses and the flats, away from The Factory and the strikers and scabs. They kept walking until they found the hills, which were still carved up with lines and circles – the purported language of The Alien.

They walked until the sun finished its day shift and gave

way to the bloated moon.

They walked until they found the place to which a cow had been led before being slaughtered.

They walked together, and that was enough for the meantime.

*

"Are you sure this is safe?" Kitty asked uncertainly. She struggled to see through her black veil, but taking it off in public would be – to her – disrespectful to the memory of her father. And yet it was getting dark very quickly; too quickly for Kitty's liking.

"Well of course it isn't safe," Porter said in what was meant to be a reassuring voice. "But we are doing something very important tonight. And perhaps…just perhaps…along the way we might meet up with a murderer. And stop him!"

Kitty couldn't see her face – no-one could – but she didn't need to see herself to know that she had just turned a sickly shade of lime green. This happened to her whenever she felt ill or scared stiff. Or, as in this instance: both!

"But I don't want to meet up with a murderer!" she snapped irritably. Irritation was another sign that she wasn't happy with her rash decision to leave the safety of her home.

"Besides, I know who is responsible for all the disappearances."

Something out of the corner of her eye moved quickly, something near enough for her to see clearly through her veil. It was the spaceboy supermodel named JFK. He seemed a little bit too trigger happy, because every time Kitty looked over at him (and she did often) he seemed to have his hand dangerously close to the gun on his hip.

"You know where The Alien is hiding? Where is it? Who has it possessed?"

"You need to speak English," she said, "and stop playing

with your gun!"

But Porter wasn't interested in JFK or his gun. He wanted an answer.

"Who is the murderer?"

"It's the Government!" Kitty declared with excitable fingers dancing as though to punctuate each letter of each word she spoke.

Both JFK and Porter laughed.

"The pathetic governments of Earth don't know what they're dealing with!" JFK said passionately. "The Alien will kill everyone until it gets the perfect body in which to conquer the universe. Not even The Federation will be able to stop it."

Porter stopped laughing and suddenly moved away from JFK. He hated it when his friend started all his spooky sci-fi nonsense; he sounded far too much like his awful parents, who lied as easily as they ate takeaway. Keeping his eyes firmly on Kitty, Porter attempted a quick change of subject:

"And why would the government want to kidnap teenagers?"

Kitty looked up at the Moon in frustration, because it was **so damn obvious**.

"They're experimenting on them!"

"Why?" Porter asked. He wasn't giving up. Kitty's theories were just as ludicrous as those of JFK, who thought he was on a secret mission to kill an alien whilst living inside a wooden spaceship. ~~Yes,~~ a voice said sardonically, ~~we're the only sane ones here.~~

"Because..." Kitty spluttered "...that's what governments do. They conduct deadly experiments on people, make destructive weapons from the remains of crashed UFOs, and they cover up alien invasions! Oh and that big fat round happy moon above us? We've never set foot on it. The entire Moon-landing was faked."

JFK's hand slid down to the gun again.

"Just what do you know about alien invasions?"

Kitty gulped loudly. She was rapidly finding JFK less and less attractive.

Porter stopped them both with a wave of his hand.

"We're here," he said quietly.

They waited for his instruction, but it wouldn't come. Porter gripped the flaky blue railings that were part of the bridge, the same bridge that cut the school off from the road that passed the hills he had come to know intimately over the last seven days. The bridge was shaped like a snake, suspended above the road, connecting the school entrance to the block of flats on nearby Hillcroft Road. JFK's 'spaceship' was nearby, which explained how he had come to see The Minters faking their rubbish crop circles at night.

But now there were other people gathered around the foot of the hills.

These were new people, the kind that Porter didn't know but instantly recognised.

"They're soldiers!" he blurted out, hating himself for stating the obvious.

"What are soldiers doing here?" asked JFK, fingers itchy to pull a trigger.

"Are you sure they're the military?" Kitty asked, with a quick lift of her funeral veil. "They might be policemen in riot gear. I've seen them before and they look like bulky soldiers. They were fighting against a riot three weeks ago outside The Factory, just up the road."

JFK assessed the situation as only a fully trained soldier from Planet 5758 could, and his evaluation backed up Porter's initial supposition.

"They move like soldiers," he said in the manner of a boy with lots of experience within the armed forces. "I think they've been sent to hunt down The Alien From Another Dimension."

"The Alien From Another Dimension?" Kitty struggled.

"That's the name of the monster kidnapping our

schoolmates."

"Are you actually for real?"

"I assure you I am being very honest and The Alien is real."

It soon became obvious what the soldiers were doing in Castlekrankie.

"They're taking the cow away!" Porter cried out in panic. No, this couldn't happen. He had to give the poor animal a proper burial. It was a powerful urge inside him, something Porter knew he *had* to do, because he owed it to the cow.

It was the closest he would get to burying one of Ma and Pa's victims. And the opportunity was being taken away, put beyond reach.

In a sudden burst of energy that startled both JFK and Kitty, Porter moved down the bridge, weaving his way with his hand on the rusted railing, moving towards the hills in a bid to get closer to the soldiers and the cow. His booted feet pounding the tarmac, he was halfway down the bridge when he heard a soft voice sigh deep inside his brain:

~~You're wrong,~~ it said sadly, ~~you have buried one of Ma and Pa's victims…you've buried me deep inside these fleshy dark places of your brain. I didn't choose to be this way!~~

*

The soldiers were already driving away by the time the three teenagers reached the site of the crop circles.

"Where are they going?" Porter yelled angrily.

"It looks like they're heading towards the Toy Shop at the other side of the forest," Kitty surmised. Though she didn't know it, she had deduced their destination correctly.

"What is the Toy Shop?" Porter asked. He didn't know anything about a 'Toy Shop'.

"It used to be a production plant for toys, but it shut down when I was in nursery. No-one goes to the Toy Shop anymore. The entire place is abandoned and derelict."

Porter couldn't understand why soldiers would steal a dead cow and take it in the direction of an old toy-making factory. But he was absolutely enthralled by the mystery!

"It seems the abandoned Toy Shop isn't abandoned anymore!" JFK added helpfully. "Those soldiers have set up a base there, for some tactical reason. We must figure out their stratagem and fight back with all the weaponry at our disposal."

Then there was an awkward pause, because Porter knew what Kitty was about to say.

He waited.

She didn't disappoint him.

*

"I *told* you it was a government conspiracy," Kitty said smugly.

BLOOD, GUTS, AND DEATH BEAMS

Kenneth Carlton was proud to lead the workers to inevitable victory over the corrupt, scummy board of directors at The Factory. As leader of the union, he knew that his voice carried the combined power and force of all the men and women who paid their dues. They looked up to him to fight against the evil greedy pigs who wanted them to work long hours without holidays or good pay.

Every worker, Kenneth would say every time he stepped up to a podium, *deserves equal pay because everyone should be treated as equals.*

So he wasn't prepared when allegations of bribery emerged thanks to a pesky reporter at the *Castlekrankie Chronicle*. Something had to be done. His honour – no, the honour of the union and the workers – was at stake!

Kenneth slicked back his blonde hair – the campest hairdo in the history of trade unionism – and emerged from the conservatory of his five-bedroom house, preparing himself for a vicious fight with the assembled reporters in the field that was his garden.

They all pounced on him as soon as they caught sight of his wispy comb-over.

One journalist – a woman whose Press ID identified her as Amanda McNab – asked cuttingly: "How do you respond to accusations of bribery and corruption?"

"It's all lies!" Kenneth Carlton said as he opened the door of his brand new Lamborghini Reventon, a black super car that looked faintly like the Batmobile.

He got inside and ripped down the road, leaving the

journalists to choke on his smoke.

*

Kenneth Carlton bristled at accusations that he was the only union leader in history who had initiated a major industrial strike living inside a flat but ended it with a large, extravagant home. He had no time for snide or cruel people who clearly didn't know the facts. Whenever someone suggested he go into politics, Kenneth laughed, because that would mean taking a savage pay cut.

He only did what he did to protect the workers and their rights.

Of course, helping people didn't preclude helping oneself.

*

The car moved down the road, past the school and the hills where...Kenneth checked the rear view mirror...it seemed as if men in uniform were packing something into a van. He noticed that the van was unregistered. Thank goodness they weren't the police! In his haste to escape the press, Kenneth hadn't fastened his seatbelt. He had an uneasy feeling that these men had something to do with The Strike. They *had* to be connected to the scum in charge of The Factory.

At that moment Kenneth watched as three stupid kids ran across the road towards the hill where the van was pulling away. He didn't know who they were, or why they were dressed so foolishly, but he peered through the windscreen in nosy fascination as one of them – a boy wearing a bad Halloween space costume – hailed a taxi.

Kenneth slowed his car and felt the power around him ebb.

"What is going on here?" he asked himself, slightly annoyed that none of his spies in The Factory had warned him about the presence of soldiers in town.

The little black cab moved cautiously after the van, as

though the passengers had instructed the driver to follow but remain unseen. Kenneth smiled at the idea of a bunch of kids tracking down soldiers without their knowing about it.

Kenneth Carlton took his eyes off the rear view mirror so he could check his hair, because he didn't want anyone to see his bald patch, then he drove his car towards the hill and the direction of the van taxi.

But it was already too late.

He had lost them both.

He was still driving when something shocking happened to him:

A little grey man stepped out in front of his car.

He looked right at Kenneth with large, unblinking oval eyes of deepest black.

Something bright flickered and dazzled Kenneth.

Blinded, he screamed – an automatic reaction – until adrenaline and instinct moved his hands over the wheel. The Alien – for Kenneth knew it had to be one – tilted its head quizzically, watching as the car whizzed off the road and plunged towards the forest.

Kenneth prayed for a soft impact as trees quickly filled the windscreen.

He spun the steering wheel.

And the world spun with him.

*

The Alien watched as the coffin on wheels smashed into a particularly hefty oak tree. The impact was enough to send its driver crashing through the windscreen, unleashing a blizzard of glass and blood and bone.

The Alien frowned, because the body was useless as a result of the injuries.

The three teenagers he had observed from the forest were now following the military towards their base of operations.

That meant The Alien had to follow them too.

The wreckage of the car glowed like dull embers. The Alien watched, spellbound by the evolution of fire. There it stood, lost to time, until the sound of sirens in the distance made it aware of the encroaching world. The Alien shivered slightly, the crisp night air carrying not only sound but another warning of winter, despite the heat of the crash.

Then The Alien did what aliens do whenever humans are in close proximity.

It disappeared.

LIFE IS UN-FARE

Joe Murdoch was on his way home from a long day of doing nothing when someone hailed his cab. The fact that people actually wanted to use his taxi was akin to a second coming, because the return of Jesus to civilisation was more likely than someone in Castlekrankie needing a cab. There was nothing worse than being a cabbie in a town with an unemployment rate of ninety-eight percent.

Being a cabbie in Castlekrankie was a thankless job and if The Strike didn't end soon, there would be no taxis left in town. Joe would need to use the new food bank.

Thank goodness for teenagers with disposable income!

*

"So where are you going?" Joe asked pleasantly, his delight for paying customers obvious. He had to tone it down because he didn't want them thinking he was a lunatic. It wasn't often he had people to talk to, so Joe wanted to make the best of this situation.

He turned to greet his three guests, but the words melted in his mouth when he finally realised who he had let into his cosy cab:

Three freak teenagers dressed in ridiculous outfits:

One of them, a boy, was dressed as a spaceman.

The other boy, who seemed to be the leader of the group, was dressed in a purple tweed jacket with clashing jeans and big boots. He also carried a handbag: an actual handbag, the sort Joe's ex-wife had carried around back when he'd actually made money as a cabbie. "I have lots of handbags," the boy grinned. "This is my second bag of the day."

The third, a girl, wore a black veil across her eyes, but everything she had on was black, from her Morticia Addams lace top to the shiny black leggings and high heels.

Her mouth was curled down into a little frown.

"Is there something wrong?" she asked quizzically.

"Is today Halloween?" Joe asked candidly.

"Every day is Halloween," the girl in the veil chuckled.

"Where do you want to go?" Joe asked, terrified that he had just accepted three serial killers into his car and into his life.

"We want you to follow those soldiers," said the boy in the spacesuit.

He looked very serious.

"If you pay me," Joe replied, "I'll follow anyone anywhere!"

*

The man in the front of the cab wore a peaked cap, the kind pensioners wore when they wanted to keep the cold off their scalp, and Porter felt the driver's striped blue-and-red jumper wasn't too ugly on the eye – but he also wore a permanent smile firmly on his face. It was wide enough to reveal metal teeth, the result of dentistry gone mad. Porter found his enthusiasm very creepy, because it reminded him of Happy Lemon Washington and her never-ending smile.

"Why are you chasing a bunch of soldiers?" Joe asked Porter.

"They stole our cow," he said simply.

"Hmm," the driver said, "how inconvenient for you."

Then he suddenly came to a surprisingly perceptive conclusion:

"Didn't aliens leave that cow on the crop circles?"

~~This man is an idiot! Please don't talk to him. You know I don't like idiots!~~

"If by 'aliens' you mean 'my parents' then yes, they left that cow on the crop circles."

"Porter's parents are crooks," JFK explained as his fingers itched for ray gun action.

"Why are you wearing that veil?" Joe asked Kitty suddenly, as he turned a corner down another long road. He seemed utterly bemused by his customers.

"I'm in mourning for the people of Castlekrankie, crushed under the heels of fat pie-making capitalists who want to steal our money and our dignity."

~~Really?~~ a mocking voice inside Porter's head exclaimed. ~~I thought it was because her dad was a dead drunk.~~

"Shut up!" Porter hissed.

"I'm sorry," Joe said stiffly, insulted by the boy with the sparkly black handbag.

"No I didn't mean you! I'm talking to the voice in my head."

But the driver said nothing else as he drove after the soldiers in the van with the cow.

*

Back in the mid-'90s, at the height of Cool Britannia, an enterprising businessman moved into Castlekrankie for his latest business venture. Having spotted a gap in the market for cheap toys, he bought an old factory near the forest – not The Factory, another factory, smaller and less significant – a place in which to make dolls that would be sold at bargain prices. The Toy Shop, as it became known, with its gaudy pink neon castle exterior, was, in reality, a boring industrial unit made to look like the stuff of fairy tales. To part the pink curtains at the door was to see ugly conveyor belts and zombified underpaid staff pinning plastic eyes into crappy plastic doll heads. The candy-floss pink walls and cream-coloured stripes made the entire building look like a deranged remix of Willy Wonka's Chocolate Factory, or a cheap concrete wedding cake.

The Toy Shop went out of production **fifty days** after it went into production.

And the place remained desolate; an old fairy-tale castle surrounded by rusty barbed wire and numerous old signs warning of the dire consequences of trespassing.

Or so it seemed.

Then a taxi arrived.

*

Porter fished his wallet from the recesses of his Dolce & Gabbana. He paid the cabbie the fare, plus a nice tip for getting them to the old abandoned military base. Joe wasn't sure he should leave the teenagers in a dilapidated dump like the Toy Shop, but he found them so weird that he didn't actually want to be around them.

It was only after he pulled away from the building that he realised something was wrong. He felt different. It took him a few minutes to realise there was something missing.

"They stole my hat!" he yelped as his hand went up to his head to feel…nothing.

It was true. His little cap was gone, lifted off his head by the girl in black.

*

Somewhere, outside in the night, Kitty Stomp sighed with happiness as she examined her brand new hat. She wouldn't wear it, that wasn't the point – it had been on someone else's (possibly unwashed) head – but she had wanted it and she hadn't been able to stop herself.

Then she saw where Porter wanted them to go.

And her happiness drifted away, leaving her feeling utterly barren.

*

"We can't go inside the Toy Shop. It looks like Barbie's Dream Meth Lab!"

But Kitty's protests fell on deaf ears.

"I want to go home," she said to Porter and JFK.

"But we need you!" Porter replied as JFK melted a hole in the wire fencing, his ray gun finally put to good use.

"Why?"

"I need someone who can steal a cow's body, and we can't do it without you. You can go home after we give the cow a proper burial, and you can leave me and JFK to find The Alien."

Then he added a late addition to his train of thought:

"Besides, I want to know why those soldiers are here in Castlekrankie."

Kitty was about to say something very rude when everything went white.

A powerful spotlight hit the three teenagers, pinning them in a circle. Porter and Kitty were too startled to do anything other than huddle in terror behind JFK.

"You had to go and jinx us!" Kitty wailed.

The sound of boots crunching on gravel was overpowering, as was the clicking of sub-machine guns, the sound of an army preparing to execute enemies on the battlefield.

"These people are intruders," a clipped voice said grandly in the night.

The soldiers waited for an order, which finally came in the form of two words.

"Kill them!"

JOHNMANIA

"You can't kill us!" Porter cried out in horror.

The voice in charge of the guns seemed amused at the idea of a teenager telling him what to do, and he didn't bother hiding it as he spoke.

"You are trespassing on government property. Why can't we shoot you?"

Porter smiled inwardly, because the soldiers had just confirmed they were using the Toy Shop as a makeshift base of operations...but for what purpose? What was in that base that they were prepared to kill for? Out loud, however, he said:

"Because...I know all about the aliens who made the crop circles on the hills."

Silence, and then whispers – excited murmuring that let Porter know he had them.

Kitty was confused. Confusion wasn't a new experience for the teenage shoplifter.

"I thought you said those crop circles were made by your mum and OUCH!"

Porter hit her shin with his handbag, instantly clearing up any confusion in Kitty's mind.

JFK nodded at the soldiers. "I can take them all out," he said with all the bravado he could muster. "Their primitive Earth weaponry is no match for my particle-beam triax death ray."

The spotlight went off before anyone could fire a gun.

And the soldiers bundled the teenagers into the old (but not abandoned) Toy Shop.

*

The inside of the Toy Shop was completely at odds with the

outside. The interior was modern and – dare Porter think it – militaristic, the opposite of the charming pink fairy-tale castle and fake wooden turrets outside. But there was something else about the base, something very familiar: the antiseptic smell reminded him of a hospital. And Porter suddenly realised he *was* being escorted through an actual hospital; and not any ordinary one, but some sort of military hospital.

But who were its patients?

*

Porter was separated from Kitty and JFK, and though he was utterly terrified, he didn't show it; he defiantly raised his handbag as the soldiers bundled him into a room.

There was a desk in the room. On the desk was a small lamp.

"Sit!" one of the voices snarled at him.

Porter idly took a seat, never once letting go of his Dolce & Gabbana.

That bag, a voice said through his left ear, is a symbol of your inherent classiness.

"Damn right," Porter agreed.

"Don't speak until you're spoken to!" A soldier waved his gun to punctuate his threat.

"What are you going to do?" Porter hissed. "Shoot me for being sickeningly amazing?"

The lamp clicked on and the light was twisted around until it found Porter's face. The light was hot and Porter felt his skin prickling under the heat, turning red, an interrogation tan. But he remained defiant, wondering how JFK and Kitty were faring.

There were three soldiers in the room; Porter knew that from their outlines. But who were they and why were they so interested in aliens?

The interrogation commenced with little fanfare:

"What do you know about the crop circles?"

"Are aliens trying to speak to us?"

"What are they trying to say?"

"Is an invasion imminent?"

"Do aliens speak to you?"

~~No, I do. Goodness, that one on the right has really bad breath!~~

"Where do these aliens come from?"

"Was the cow a message?"

"Was it some sort of weird alien sacrifice to their unearthly gods?"

After twenty minutes of being interrogated, Porter decided he couldn't take any more of it. So he simply smiled and asked a question of the nearest soldier:

"Hello. What is your name?"

The soldier – they all looked the same to Porter, but he supposed that was the point of uniforms – backed away from the table slightly and replied gruffly: "My name is John."

Porter looked at the second soldier in the room, the one in the middle of the khaki-clad trio. "Good. And what is your name?"

The soldier waited for a few seconds before answering.

"My name is John."

~~This is getting a bit weird. I bet the third soldier's name is John.~~

"Is your name John as well?" Porter asked the third soldier.

He smiled thinly, a mouth barely visible in the glare.

"My name is John."

Porter looked at the three interchangeable soldiers and came to the conclusion that they were a perfect metaphor for the military. And then he wondered, with a pang of worry, where JFK and Kitty were and whether they were safe or not.

"You need to tell us what you know about the alien threat!"

~~The Three Stooges have started again!~~

"What are those crop circles on the hills?"

"Are they the landing patterns of a spaceship?"

"Is there a secret invasion being planned?"

~~And the letter of the day kids is 'C' for Cretin, Clod, Chump and...~~

Porter decided this was getting him nowhere, so he grabbed the lamp and twisted the spotlight around until it shone in the face of his main interrogator, the nearest John.

~~...And...~~

Spurred on by his second voice, Porter stood up and swung his handbag at the first soldier, smacking him full on, with enough power to send him crumpling to the ground. The two remaining Johns reacted more quickly than Porter, however, and brought their machine guns up, training them on him before he could raise his bag again.

"Custard," Porter said, as he looked down at the unconscious John on the floor, custard from broken cans all around him. Porter didn't like getting his expensive bag grimy, but now he knew it was a potential fake, like all the others he had been gifted over the years, ruining it mattered less.

~~Oh yes that's a good one!~~

Then the room rumbled – the ominous vibration of a local earthquake passed through everyone. Porter couldn't believe it. There was no way an earthquake could be happening right now, not in a town like Castlekrankie. The two Johns seemed slightly alarmed too, wearing almost identical expressions of confusion on almost identical faces.

Porter tracked the source of the vibration to the door behind the soldiers. Something immensely powerful was smashing the door.

"If military intelligence is an oxymoron, as some people say, then you two are the biggest morons of all! There is NO alien invasion! My parents faked those crop circles because they're con artists who want to exploit the disappearances of teenagers in town. There is a psycho on the loose and he's responsible for kidnap and, I'll bet, murder too. And one more thing – please pay attention because this is important...**Give me back my dead cow!"**

Then the door exploded open, razed by superior firepower, the sound of which made Porter jump in fright. He saw a figure in white fill the doorway, and a face he was delighted to see again. The soldiers, however, weren't happy to see him at all.

They raised their guns menacingly.

"Watch out, JFK!" Porter yelled hoarsely.

JFK was quicker than the two remaining Johns, flicking up his right hand and firing before either soldier had the chance to react. Porter could only stand aside and watch as sparks punched both soldiers onto the ground.

"They had better not be dead!" Porter cried out as he ran past JFK.

"My particle-beam triax pistol is on the stun setting."

"In other words you didn't use proper fireworks for your flare gun?"

A girl in black soon joined Porter and JFK, but Porter didn't recognise her.

"Do I know you?"

"It's me," she said in exasperation, "Kitty Stomp!"

Then she put on her hat, complete with black funeral veil across her eyes.

"I recognise you now!" Porter smiled.

"We're going to get your cow and then we're going to find The Alien. Okay?" JFK said firmly. He was desperate to track down his enemy, and he was clearly having second thoughts about Porter's plans.

But Porter wasn't listening.

He had just found something odd.

It was a door to another section of the Toy Shop.

"JFK," he started, "what planet do you come from?"

"I come from Planet 5758."

The door in front of Porter was labelled 5758.

THE CASTLEKRANKIE SLEEPERS

Sirens suddenly exploded into life, flooding the building with noise and movement. Someone – probably one of the Johns – had activated the alarm and now everyone knew the three teenagers were on the loose.

"We need to get out of here fast," Kitty said, straining to be heard over the klaxons.

"Shall we go in here?" Porter asked. Secretly, he really wanted to turn the handle and discover what lay behind Door 5758. He couldn't explain it but Porter had the oddest feeling that JFK's fate lay behind the door, and that he was somehow unknowingly connected to the secret operation going on inside the Toy Shop. He had no proof, other than his gut instinct, but his suspicion was more than enough to drive him.

"We have to decide!"

"Let's do it," Kitty said to both of them.

JFK seemed reluctant. His face was furrowed into a frown, as though he was trying to remember something important. Porter could see something stirring deep inside JFK, a battle of sorts. He wanted to go through the door, but fear was stopping him.

Porter made the decision himself.

He grabbed JFK and Kitty by the hands and together they passed through the door.

What they found was so astounding that Porter's second voice gasped in shock.

*

The door was an entrance into a large hanger filled with beds.

"It IS a hospital," Porter said excitedly.

Each bed was occupied by a body and each body was hooked up to a machine, with an array of thick tubes guiding chemicals from the machine into the patient. There was a slight vibration in the background and the choir of tubular lights on the ceiling buzzed as one, while the dialysis machines bleeped softly at different rates.

But there was another sound, a quite distinctive one that each teenager recognised:

It was the sound of snoring; a symphony of snorts and snuffles.

"They're *all* asleep!" Kitty whispered, though her version of a whisper was still loud.

Porter, JFK, and Kitty walked down the centre of the room. It took a little while for them to reach the other side, it was so far from the door.

Porter looked around the room for information. He exuded a nervous energy.

"There *has* to be a medical clipboard somewhere nearby," he told his two friends. "Then we can figure out what's wrong with these men." It didn't take Porter long to track one down. It lay on a side cabinet by one of the central beds. It was crammed with pages of handwritten notes; but some of the scribbled writing was so bad that it was almost another language. Porter lifted it up and looked over it, turning pages he didn't understand until he found something he did; a signature and a long, overly-complicated diagnosis.

"Professor Wrathorga," he told the others, "has been experimenting on something called 'biofeedback therapy'… and no, I don't have the foggiest idea what that phrase means. But it looks like he forced these soldiers into a group coma after his experiment went wrong."

Kitty seemed perversely thrilled by the prospect of a mad scientist being involved:

"I bet mad scientists are lurking around here somewhere,

conducting their evil experiments as part of the government conspiracy," she declared grandly.

"No," Porter retorted, sick of hearing about conspiracies and other mumbo jumbo. "It seems he was trying to *help* the soldiers. These men have served in different military situations – wars and skirmishes around the world – and none of them could sleep afterwards. There's a reference here to vivid nightmares." He snatched another clipboard and frantically went through the diagnosis. "Each patient in this room volunteered for some sort of experimental treatment for dream manipulation. I bet they all suffered from post-traumatic stress disorder."

Porter fell into an uneasy silence, before finally adding:

"This is completely unethical."

*

POST-TRAUMATIC STRESS DISORDER is a serious psychological condition that can cause flashbacks, guilt, problems with concentration, and chronic insomnia. Post-traumatic stress disorder usually occurs after an upsetting experience such as military combat, violence, abuse, injury, or prolonged exposure to episodes of *Happy Lemontown*.

*

"Are you okay, JFK?" Kitty asked. She was concerned for her new friend. His skin was the colour of sour lemon sherbet. Kitty knew this because she had recently pinched a box of Sour Lemon Sherbet from Planet Pound.

"I know this place," he told her. "How do I know this place?"

"Maybe you were a soldier who escaped?" Porter offered. That was his latest theory and it helped explain a great many mysteries about JFK; not only did he seem to understand the ways of the armed forces, but he also had access to weaponry that someone his age ought not to have. Both suggested to Porter that JFK had taken his arsenal from the base.

"I *am* a soldier. I come from Planet 5758 in the constellation of Hypo Sot. I'm here to stop The Alien From Another Dimension completing its plans for world domination."

~~Hypo Sot? Is that an anagram of…? Yes! It all fits!~~

Porter didn't get angry, but he was quickly losing his patience, a feeling he hated.

"But none of that is real, JFK. You've been fed that rubbish by someone…and I know how that feels…but you must be rational about such things! You are not a spaceman from another world."

~~And you aren't in a position to lecture anyone about their sanity.~~

"Shut up or I'll triple the power of the rainbow."

~~Your medication has no power over me. I will be free!~~

"Hey!" Kitty yelled. "Hey! I know this man."

She was pointing at a patient snoring away on a bed.

"Is he one of our classmates?"

"No," Kitty told Porter, shooting down another one of his theories. "It's Bert Callaghan. He's one of the strikers who helped my dad in the union. He was outside The Factory every day until one day he didn't show up. We just assumed he'd run off with Mrs Donnelly from the bakery."

Porter was utterly perplexed. What was a man doing in an army hospital when he wasn't part of the army? None of this made sense to him. And he certainly didn't believe there was a government conspiracy linked to The Strike. No, there had to be another explanation; something that linked the soldiers to the strikers to the missing teenagers to JFK's hunt for an alien serial killer; a chain that bound them all together.

"I need to make the connection," Porter told himself.

And 'himself' in the voice of his brother answered back:

~~Then will you open the suitcase and free me?~~

While Porter was deep in a heated debate with his other personality, Kitty decided to explore the room further, and it wasn't long before she found something that didn't fit into the decor, something that didn't belong in a hospital ward.

An enormous wooden bookshelf filled with books.

None of which were medical tomes.

Kitty's face lit up under the veil and she felt the thrill of something new to plunder.

When Porter and JFK found Kitty, she was robbing the bookshelf.

"Put those back!" Porter hissed, his handbag quivering slightly.

But Kitty was revelling in the opportunity to add a hoard of books to her collection of stolen goods. She literally knocked books off the shelf, knocking them with precision into her bag of robbed junk.

"It's like being in the Waiting Room and seeing all those old books and magazines piled up! All mime for the taking! The Professor has a really good collection. He has the *Nancy Drew Mystery Series*, an Agatha Christie or two…oh my giddy aunt…I've just found some crappy James Patterson novels. I'll put those back. Oooh, he has some *Three Investigators* books too. Fantastic! I'll take those and I'll take those and those…"

But one pesky book – a copy of *Twilight* – refused to budge, which was inconvenient.

Kitty tugged harder, and then yanked violently until the book came off the shelf.

That's when the entire bookshelf slid away to reveal a secret room.

~~Zoiks!~~

DARK SCIENCE

It was a hidden laboratory, an extension of the hospital wing, but one which instantly felt grimier and nastier. It looked less like a hospital and more like a torture chamber. An intense all-pervading feeling of evil was palpable, but JFK felt it more intensely than his two friends. He felt he knew this place. He shivered as he walked into the room, followed by Porter and finally Kitty.

There were two beds in the room. Both had straps on them. Kitty examined them to see what she could steal.

"This one is stained... What *is* that on the bed?"

She ran a finger over a stain and instantly went rigid with horror and disgust.

"It's blood!" she croaked as her throat tightened in disgust. "And it's fresh."

Porter eagerly ransacked the room for clues. He had a horrible feeling about the secret laboratory Kitty had accidentally uncovered. JFK stood motionless by the bed, struggling with his unreliable memory.

"Someone has been here recently!" Kitty added, because she wasn't convinced the others were taking her latest grisly discovery at all seriously. "A mad scientist is carving up people in Castlekrankie!"

Porter opened a filing cabinet that hadn't been locked, thankfully, and found something close to an actual clue. The files solved another mystery:

Kitty was right. Professor Wrathorga was conducting illegal experiments.

"I knew there had to be a mad scientist involved in this weirdness," Kitty said.

Porter wasn't listening, because he was busy going through files. He was trying his hardest to speed read and find a way of explaining JFK, the military, and the sleepers.

And what he found was terrifying.

*

From what Porter could read, the files told the full story of research by Professor Milo Wrathorga into helping traumatised soldiers sleep.

"I think I saw him outside the school gates," Kitty said, "but I assumed he was just an old perv." She wrinkled her nose in disgust at a photograph of him, with his little piggy eyes and grey unkempt hair and beard.

Porter read on. Some soldiers, after returning from various stints in warzones across the world, couldn't sleep because of the nightmares and flashbacks. Their dreams were overwhelming, and The Professor, in his benevolence, wanted to stop the dreaming. By preventing the nightmares he could help the soldiers and let them lead normal lives again.

But at some point he had stopped helping them, and started hurting them instead.

Each patient had a file.

Each file was in the rusty green filing cabinet.

But there were extra files that didn't belong to soldiers.

"I recognise some of these faces," Porter said to Kitty as he thumbed through the recent records. Professor Wrathorga had been very scrupulous in his filing system, compiling information about each and every patient.

And that included many who didn't want to be there in the first place.

One of the faces in the many photographs of dead teenagers belonged to Alfie.

Porter closed his eyes and sighed, because he had known this was going to happen at some point. His search for Alfie had now become a quest for revenge. But that didn't make him feel any better – yet another person he had failed. Porter felt sick with sadness.

After a few seconds quietly contemplating his revenge, Porter looked at the file again.

"Professor Wrathorga's research into dreams and sleep involved virtual reality simulations, and daily injections of drugs with names I won't try to pronounce," Porter said aloud. The complicated medical jargon was making his head spin. "The Professor also removed cranial fluids – I think that means he took stuff out of their brains – but the treatment went wrong."

"What happened?" JFK asked flatly. He really wanted to shoot something.

"Instead of helping the soldiers to sleep without dreaming, he **stopped** them sleeping completely. Can you imagine what it must feel like to never ever sleep? The volunteer soldiers became too aggressive after the experiments."

But that didn't explain one important thing that Kitty didn't understand.

"Why is Bert out there? He's a striker, not a soldier."

"I think the Professor must have felt terribly guilty for what he did, so getting a cure at any cost became his obsession. According to his notes..." (Porter flicked through sheets of paper until he found the relevant page) "...the army cut his funding and he no longer had any volunteers. He writes here that he has started paying money out of his life savings to those strikers willing to take part in his medical trials."

Kitty's eyes lit up in sudden understanding.

"The riots and the violence suddenly got really bad under a year ago! Maybe the Professor aimed for The Strike to be blamed for the sudden surge of violence in town? He paid them for their service, changed them, took notes and sent them away."

"But why did The Professor become so unstable? How did

he go from helping the men to killing people?" JFK asked, his fingers moving towards one of the pistols holstered at his hip. The desire to destroy the lab was almost too strong to resist.

"Some of these later files are very erratic. The Professor talks about being abducted by aliens and blaming an alien for what happened to the sleepers. I suspect he suffered a nervous breakdown, and for some reason he was allowed to continue his experiments unchecked. The lunatic was in charge of the asylum."

~~Hasn't everyone taken a nervous breakdown at some point? Maybe I suffered a nervous breakthrough. I don't know what to think. It echoes inside your skull.~~

Kitty had a question, perhaps the most pertinent question of all:

"Why kidnap and kill people from school? Is he killing them and harvesting their bits for science? Is this a Burke and Hare situation?"

Porter lifted one last file. It was the most important one.

"I don't think The Professor is our serial kidnapper."

*

The file had one photograph inside it.

It was the battered, bloodied, dead face of Professor Wrathorga.

The date was marked as eight months ago.

Whoever was behind the kidnapping and killing of teenagers of Castlekrankie, it certainly wasn't a mad scientist.

Someone had already dealt with The Professor.

And they were still out there.

Waiting.

ESCAPE FROM THE TOY SHOP

There was a door in the laboratory, which led to the outside of the Toy Shop.

The three teenagers gave each other mock salutes and cheered their escape. They would finally be able to outwit the soldiers currently on the hunt for them. Porter noticed JFK was slightly sullen, probably depressed after being confronted with evidence that he wasn't an actual space pilot, but a teenager who suffered....well, he couldn't remember.

But first there was the matter of liberating a cow's corpse.

*

The remains of an innocent cow, slaughtered by Ma and Pa for their ridiculous con, lay outside the base on a large wooden pallet. It had a large metal crank underneath, with wheels and a handle, useful for pulling.

The alarms wailed loudly around the three teenagers as they ran towards the cow.

"We need a plan of action right now!" Porter huffed and puffed.

"This is where I come in useful," Kitty said in a knowledgeable manner, excited to finally put her expertise to use. She had already identified two ways of escape, and directed Porter and JFK down the concrete tarmac towards the side of the base. The spotlight didn't reach that part of the fence. It was ideal for concealment.

But Porter wasn't having any of it.

"What's wrong with it?" Kitty said petulantly.

Porter didn't reply, except to point down at the ground.

Kitty looked and found...cracks on the pavement.

"Really?"

"I have Obsessive Compulsive Disorder when it comes to broken pavements!"

Kitty sighed and pushed the cow towards the back of the base. It would take a bit longer, and it was riskier, but at least there she couldn't see cracks on the pavement.

"I'm going to call this cow Happy Lemon," Porter said solemnly as he pushed the wooden pallet across the tarmac.

"You're naming it after the children's TV presenter?" JFK asked. "Why?"

Porter pointed at the cow's face.

"They look exactly like each other. Can't you see it?"

JFK was about to reply when two soldiers found them.

*

"Are you actually stealing a dead cow?" one of the two soldiers asked incredulously.

"I want to give it a proper burial," Porter protested meekly.

~~You can't bring me back by righting every wrong our parents do.~~

"I just want to make sure someone says goodbye to it," Porter added sadly.

"You are wanted for questioning," the other soldier said, while raising his gun.

"What is your name?" Kitty barked at them in her best impression of a Sergeant Major.

"That's classified information."

"I bet they're both called John," Porter said drily.

JFK was about to say something when his entire body became rigid, his face freezing into a grimace. The spotlight beam covered the wall close to where they had exited the laboratory, but there was something else on the wall. It came from the darkness, hidden from light and everything else, but JFK felt it instinctively.

"He's here," he said between gritted teeth.

"Who?" Porter asked, instantly noticing a change in JFK's body language.

"The Alien From Another Dimension."

"The killer is here?" Kitty squealed fearfully.

"Yes," snarled JFK. "I can feel its presence."

The two soldiers didn't know what the three teens were talking about; indeed they had no inclination to talk any further. They moved towards Porter with their guns aloft. But Porter was no longer engaged in a discussion with the soldiers.

There was a shadow on the wall.

The figure casting the shadow was blotted out by the light, so he or she remained obscured.

But Porter had a flashback to the night he'd seen The Alien murdering a teenager near the old shopping district. He knew instinctively that JFK was right. The Alien was close.

Porter realised with shock that he *recognised* the moving outline.

"That shadow…I've seen it before!"

Kitty didn't seem convinced by Porter's admission, and she let it show:

"You actually recognise a person's shadow?"

Porter didn't reply, because something was niggling at the nub of his brain. He couldn't quite work out what had unsettled him so much, but something wasn't right.

One of the soldiers turned to the other and ordered him to investigate.

"Make sure they don't come back to this base," he added threateningly.

The soldier saluted and moved into the darkness, towards the spotlight that was blinding everyone. Porter cursed his bad luck at not having his expensive Ray Ban sunglasses with him, because they would have been perfect for this problem. He was getting tired of having bright lights – and guns – shoved in his face.

The soldier had only been gone for a few seconds when the sound of his scream reached the teenagers, their dead cow, and the remaining soldier.

"What the hell is going on?" the soldier demanded, his voice quivering slightly.

The tell-tale sound of gunfire erupted, blotting out the klaxons.

The screaming returned, blending in with the siren, a horrible duet. Then the scream suddenly, and violently, stopped. The wailing of the alarms continued, much to the discomfort of Kitty, who felt the pressure of a migraine building behind her eyes.

The shadow reappeared, craning along the wall as The Alien stole towards the group.

The remaining soldier guarding the teenagers fired his gun, but the bullets ricocheted across the pink-painted wall and solid-stone ground, causing yet more cracks. One bullet shattered the spotlight, plunging the base into darkness.

Porter screeched as cracks split the pavement towards his feet.

The soldier ran into the night to find his comrade, gun blazing as he chased after a shadow. He wasn't gone long before something murdered him noisily. His cries of pain didn't last as long as the previous soldier's, but they were horrific all the same.

"We need to help him!" Kitty cried vainly, fingers in her ears to blot out the horror.

"He's gone," JFK said, his ray gun unsheathed, "another victim of the war."

There was an eerie calmness. Even the klaxon had stopped.

The teenagers were suddenly alone.

But not for long.

It giggled. That was how they knew it was there with them. It was the giggle of someone who found pain and agony amusing. It didn't sound human at all. The giggle became a hideous vicious laugh. The laughter seemed to come from different angles, moving swiftly around the trio.

Someone, or *something*, was deliberately trying to frighten Porter and his friends.

"Leave us alone!" Kitty screamed.

"You're going to get what you deserve," Porter called out into the night.

JFK aimed and fired three hot sparks from the barrel of his gun.

The mocking alien laughter distorted into a scream of hate and pain.

And then it was gone.

FUNERAL FOR A COW

Porter, JFK and Kitty were emotionally and physically exhausted. After escaping through a gap in the wire fence surrounding the Toy Shop – a hole JFK widened with his ray gun – they pushed, pulled, tugged and yelled until the cow's corpse was far away from the klaxons and soldiers.

The trio moved in silence until Porter suddenly stopped.

"This is where the funeral will take place," he said solemnly.

They were back at the hill, where the crop circles had been carved, where the cow had been dumped like unwanted trash.

But Porter had another surprise for JFK and Kitty.

Two shovels fell at their feet – their handles retractable, making them easier to fit into a handbag.

"Dig," he said.

Kitty looked up sharply at her friend. Not because she resented digging into a hill in the middle of the night. And not because she didn't like being ordered around.

She was taken aback because Porter's voice sounded like it belonged to someone else.

"Dig," he repeated.

*

Once the digging had been completed, and the cow placed into the makeshift hole, the ceremony could finally begin. Something in Porter itched for it to happen. He had to do this, and for now nothing else mattered.

It was a short service, punctuated by weeping from Kitty, who sniffled and coughed throughout the improvised reading. At one point JFK put his arm around Kitty's shoulders, drawing her into his chest. As a soldier from another world, he had seen death many times before…but this was different, or at least it felt different.

"Dear Cow," Porter said sombrely, "I only knew you for a few minutes but I knew as soon as I met you in my living room that you were the nicest and most trustworthy cow a boy could meet. You aren't the first innocent to fall at the feet of my gross parents, but you'll definitely be the last. Ashes to ashes, funk to funky."

"Hallelujah!" Kitty cheered.

"Hallelujah?" JFK asked with incomprehension.

"Kumbaya my lord?" Kitty shrugged her shoulders, which was the signal for JFK to release his grip. She had no idea what she was doing at this funeral. She couldn't stand funerals, having recently had to endure her father's. But he had not been a religious man and his service had had none of the usual religious ephemera. This was a burial on a hill marked with crop circles.

For a few minutes, silence was all the hill had to offer.

And then the teenagers went their separate ways.

*

The Spirit of the Elevator was alive and in a foul mood by the time Porter reached Beckham Block. Too tired to climb the stairs, he resigned himself to using the lift. The Spirit did everything but swear at him as he pressed the button to take him up to his level. Porter honestly couldn't believe that artificial intelligences could be so petty.

I am back and I'm going to make sure it takes an extra minute to reach Ground Floor tomorrow morning!

"I'm not interested."

Do you think you can get away with vandalising my guts?

"I'm not interested."

I had the misfortune of having your parents and their friend in me earlier tonight!

And suddenly Porter was interested.

"My parents have no friends, so who was with them?"

The Spirit laughed as Porter fled the elevator and headed towards his flat.

*

The first thing Porter was confronted with was a familiar sound of sobbing, similar to the sound he'd just left. But this wasn't like Kitty's loud melodramatic sobs; it was quiet, reticent. It was the sound of someone trying not to cry in front of an audience.

Porter crept to the door of the living room and listened to the conversation:

"Jim told me that you are frauds. He says my Cassie wasn't taken by aliens but by one of the strikers, because he went back to work..."

"If aliens aren't real then why are there crop circles on the hill?"

"Why have so many people just vanished without a trace?"

"You must know that murderers leave traces of their victims..."

"But aliens with spaceships leave only one sign."

"Crop circles!"

Ma and Pa sounded like a very seductive double act, each agreeing with the other, pushing their shared agenda onto someone clearly deep in grief. Porter knew that the woman wouldn't fall for it. No-one could be that gullible. And yet he also knew from past experience that some people *are* that gullible.

There was a time you believed everything they told you.

Porter kept his mouth shut and his ears open.

"Can you really communicate with these aliens?"

"Yes!" Ma replied instantly.

"But...we need money."

"Jim said you were trying to con everyone and if you were serious about helping us, you wouldn't ask to be paid."

Porter grinned. This woman was no imbecile.

"But in order to communicate with the aliens, we need the proper equipment!"

"Technology can be expensive."

"We aren't using the internet to contact the aliens."

"No, we're using proper electrical equipment, complicated stuff."

"Which we need to pay for, and we can't do it without your help!"

"If you love your daughter, then you'll help us help you…"

"And we need a few grand!"

"Cassie is out there somewhere in space, waiting for you to tell her you miss her!"

Porter wrapped his hand around the door handle, readying himself to storm into the living room and SCREAM at the mother that his parents were liars. But his eyes fell upon something in the kitchen, placed out of sight so the grieving guest couldn't see it. He was at the right angle to see the edge of it, and it made him release the door handle and investigate. He felt his guts tighten.

He already knew what he would find. Worse, he knew what it meant.

The rusty old lawnmower sat in the corner, complete with tins of custard arranged neatly on the worktop above it.

Ma and Pa were going to start up again.

Porter would never be free of them until he did something to stop them forever.

*

The living room door opened and the voices became louder.

"I haven't been able to sleep for weeks," the woman's voice said from the hall. "My bosses have me on these energy pills to keep me awake. I'm so stressed with Cassie's disappearance and all the phone calls I've been receiving..."

"We'll take all that stress away from you," Pa said smugly.

Porter suddenly realised he recognised the woman's voice.

He peeked out from the kitchen and felt his jaw drop in amazement.

The grieving mother whose daughter had gone missing, the woman on energy pills because she was tired at work, the latest victim of Ma and Pa's scam:

It was Miss Happy Lemon Washington.

SPACESHIPS & HEAD TRIPS

The addiction was powerful and even though Connor Clarkson knew it was wrong...it felt too good to give up. He knew that as he stood amongst the group of mournful people, an intruder who didn't share their grief, though he pretended to feel it.

The wind whipped up and cold hit Connor, passing through his black woollen coat and red scarf. He had hidden his schoolbag in the church so he could safely retrieve it later, but for now he allowed thoughts of what was to come to keep him warm.

A feast! he thought voraciously. *Loads of food and I'll eat it all and feel strong again.*

The vicar's voice floated by the crowd, underneath the sounds of sobbing, until it reached Connor, giving him a sign that the service was nearly over.

Since rising, Connor had already attended three funerals, and he would go to another after this one.

Connor wasn't addicted to drugs, violence, smoking or stealing.

He was addicted to funerals!

But it wasn't the funerals that kept him coming back for more.

It was the food he got to eat afterwards, at the wake.

"Amen," the vicar said as his dog peed on a nearby gravestone.

*

The wake was held in a pub called the Devil's Dumplings and unfortunately it wasn't a lavish affair. Connor couldn't hide the disappointment from his face as he saw the pub's interior. It was a shabby old fashioned place that reeked of cigarettes and cider, the stench of which had embedded itself in the torn leather seats and russet wooden panelling. The pub was the only place that remained open on the main street; the shop across the road had been long deserted; a phony psychic with a terribly false Irish accent had operated from there, giving dire predictions of death and the end of the world to anyone stupid enough to pay him for his services.

Connor sat by the window, ignoring a speech about the latest dead person in Castlekrankie, and wondered if the owner of the psychic shop now spent his time drinking away his sorrows in the pub he must have seen every day when he closed up.

The reflection in the glass window, dirty and slick with black mould, looked back at him.

I look terrible, Connor thought as the skinny ginger-haired boy blinked back.

Then the speech ended and the food was brought out.

I'm going to eat the lot! Pies and chips and cakes and sandwiches…different flavours, fillings, textures of beef and chicken with hot gravy dripping…YUM!

Only a few of the mourners in their depressing black outfits tutted as Connor barged past them to reach the catering table.

"Didn't his mother teach him manners?"

"Who is he anyway?"

"He must be…he must have been a friend of Cally."

Connor didn't reply because he hadn't actually known Cally. She'd been two years above him at school, and when she'd gone missing…he'd smiled: another disappearance meant another funeral…and another after-funeral feast.

The table was covered in bowls and dishes brimming with pasta and chicken, as well as chipped black plates that supported towers of sandwiches and crisps. Connor eagerly snatched bits from each plate, for his own plate.

It was when he picked up a rather tasty-looking Marlowe Meat Pie that Connor heard a curious exchange from two unseen women behind him:

"I've never been to a service where there's been no body to be buried or cremated."

"You know what Sarah's like...she thinks Cally won the battle to enter heaven...and a mother apparently knows these things. She's convinced Cally isn't coming back."

"So *is* the poor dear actually dead?"

"Sarah believes so, and she's a loony...I mean, have you seen her new kitchen wallpaper? Only an unhinged mind would mix orange and red together. Was she inspired by her socks? My eyes burn every time I drink coffee in it."

"If Cally isn't dead then where is she?"

There was a pause before the reply:

"I heard she was abducted by aliens."

*

Connor felt sick as he left the Devil's Dumplings. He had eaten too much, especially given what he'd consumed earlier in the day, and now his belly felt bulbous and unsympathetic to his every step. It was dark outside and random gusts of litter slid past him, guided by the whims of the wind. The aftertaste of Marlowe Meat Pies came to him in a large burp, which he let loose in the middle of the street, down from the pub. The pressure on his stomach dissipated and he quickened his pace.

That's when he remembered that he'd left his schoolbag at the church.

"Bollocks," he said aloud as he changed direction and headed away from home again.

A few minutes passed uneventfully as Connor walked through the Art Park, which was all but abandoned in the

165

curfew. It had been a bright idea of the local cultural authority, but had gone badly wrong when The Strike had started. It was a place for creativity, communication, and abominable displays of public art. The Art Park, of all the parks in Castlekrankie, was by far the worst.

Connor had no idea someone was watching him from nearby.

*

To enter the Art Park was to take a trip through a garden of insanity.

Trees were triangular, surgically altered to be more 'challenging' in shape. The benches were white vacuumed plastic and vaguely resembled meringue shells; nobody sat on them, because people slid off, landing on the hard pavement. The benches had been designed for visual appreciation and not functionality. The water in the stream was meant to be a place for coins to be thrown, like the wishing well at the nearby shopping mall, except that people were so poor they couldn't afford to throw coins.

Even wishing was too expensive for Castlekrankie.

The concrete paths were painted yellow in a reference to the Wizard of Oz. The paths all led to the entrance and exit of the Art Park, not to anywhere useful such as a public toilet because none existed within the park's twisted iron fence. The artist who had created the area had been too busy considering his art to remember to add a toilet.

Which meant visitors used the park itself as a toilet. Some in Castlekrankie considered that apt.

*

Connor was by a large green rectangular structure – he didn't actually know what it was meant to be – when he heard something in the night.

He turned around but couldn't see anyone. It didn't help that the lights in the Art Park kept changing colour, creating a sickening psychedelic nightmare for visitors to enjoy. The grass seemed to shift from green to harsh red then white and blue then pink. The lights never stopped, which suggested to Connor that the curators had forgotten to turn them off. Either that or they didn't care about the electricity bill anymore.

Connor was nearly out of the park when he stopped to admire a statue. It was small and grey but the eyes were curiously alive, which was a remarkable design feat. Connor leaned in closer to get a look at the little grey statue.

*

The statue turned and looked right at him.

Connor fell back in disbelief. He let out a little scream of fright.

The statue raised a gloved hand and thrust it at Connor.

Something glittered.

Connor saw a supernova in the sky, an explosion of colour, and the little grey statue jumped off its plinth, moving towards him. It was incredibly fast, and for some reason it seemed to flicker and blur. Connor threw up the contents of his four dinners.

As he spat out the last drops of bile and tried to escape, Connor realised his breathing was ragged and inconstant, and that his legs wouldn't work properly as he moved as fast as he could out of the park.

That's when the spaceship arrived.

It was squat and silver, with a window on the front and powerful lights, which held their own against those of the Art Park. Red and blue and white beams danced silently across the sculptures and weird trees.

There was no-one in the cockpit of the ship.

Connor couldn't believe it. How could a spaceship move

without a pilot? It was like a car moving without a driver. It didn't make sense.

Nothing made sense except something he'd heard earlier that day:

"I heard she was abducted by aliens."

*

The last thing Connor heard before he fell was a harsh throaty laugh.

And then he was gone.

SOUTH OF NEVER

Porter lay in bed, staring at the white ceiling. He couldn't sleep. He felt weak and weary; every time he closed his eyes, aliens and spaceships and the faces of missing teenagers whirled around in a colourful vortex.

None of it made sense to him. And, like a UFO, the pieces of the puzzle went over his head; or, as his parents often said snidely whenever he didn't understand something, went North of Porter.

And yet there was something deep inside his memory, and it niggled at him, trying to be noticed among all the background noise in his skull.

"I'm missing something obvious," Porter said quietly to the ceiling.

~~Something isn't quite right...but I'm damned if I know what!~~

What had created such uneasiness in him? Something wasn't yet ready to bloom in his brain. The moment of revelation, the big twist in the tale...it just wasn't happening for him.

Porter closed his eyes and finally fell asleep.

*

The final day of school for the week was always going to be the toughest, because Porter felt that his time would be better served trying to find The Alien. But in the end he decided to go, if only to catch up with Kitty. Besides, JFK's spaceship was virtually school property, so he would be within easy reach of it.

Dressed like Jimi Hendrix, complete with a velvet suit and frilly shirt, Porter grabbed one of his many expensive Dolce & Gabbana bags and headed towards school. Being ridiculed didn't bother Porter, because he would rather people remembered him after he was long gone. And knowing his parents, he would be leaving Castlekrankie very soon.

~~We have to stop them!~~

"What can we do?" Porter asked bitterly as he walked down streets lined with soon-to-be-beautiful cherry blossom trees. The trees, Porter thought idly, might be the only bit of real beauty in Castlekrankie. The stormy wind would make the petals dance when the spring conquered winter. Porter wrapped his white scarf around himself tightly. Velvet, sadly, wasn't good against cold.

A further shock awaited him when he reached his first (and last) lesson of the day.

*

Modern Studies – an irrelevant subject in Porter's humble opinion – had a turnout of three. That didn't include his teacher, who checked the register twice just in case he'd miscounted. But each time he tallied up three pupils. It was worse than the last day of term, he told them. At least then a good dozen had turned up.

Porter surveyed the desks with a perplexed expression.

Kitty Stomp, complete with her black funeral veil, waggled her fingers in a happy wave when she realised he too was at school. She moved seats to be closer to him.

They both looked over to the third pupil in class.

It was Princess Jasmine of Planet Pound. She was not amused. Dressed like Princess Di of Castlekrankie High, with diamonds all around her white dress and expensive coat, she nonetheless sat with a dark expression that matched her true personality.

"Where *is* everyone?" Kitty asked.

"They're probably away to the food bank," Jasmine said tartly.

"They can't *all* be victims of The Alien?" Porter gasped. He knew the psycho in town was productive, but it was only now that he'd seen first-hand the effect of the disappearances on school attendance that he realised The Alien was abducting at least two people a night, if not more.

Princess Jasmine, however, didn't appear to understand a word Porter uttered.

"My father's business is under attack from a dirty thief!"

She looked at Kitty snidely:

"And for once I'm not referring to you!"

"Who is this thief you're so narked about?"

"The House of Chicken or whatever they're calling it."

Both Kitty and Porter had no idea what Princess Jasmine was referring to, so they just sat in silence, which wasn't difficult in a classroom of exactly four people.

"It's what everyone's calling the damn food bank!" Jasmine seethed, as her well-manicured hand clutched pearls around her neck. *Real pearls*, Kitty thought enviously. They would look great in her collection of stolen stuff.

"Why is it called the House of Chicken?"

"Because some rich bitch donated loads of fresh meat and fried chicken to the food bank. My dad thinks it's a filthy leftie trying to help the poor. It is a scandal. A complete scandal and a perversion of the natural order…if you want food, you work for it, right?"

"I steal it," Kitty said, with a shrug of her shoulders. She was getting bored of Princess Jasmine and her rehearsed rants, all fed to her by Daddy. In fact she really wished Jasmine wasn't at school, because Kitty really wanted to talk to Porter about what had happened the previous night. She also wanted very badly to see JFK again.

Even Jasmine noticed Kitty sighing happily.

Then their teacher started the lesson, which was to be an exciting talk about 'global security', a topic none of them had any interest in whatsoever.

Porter decided at that moment to start his own battle.

He stood up and left the room, his handbag firmly in his grip.

"Come back here!" their teacher yelled angrily. "You will be expelled!"

Porter's mocking laughter was his reply.

*

Porter crossed the school playground, all but obliterated by a heavy blanket of luminous fresh white snow, and made his way in the direction of JFK's spaceship. He had a few ideas as to what they could do next to track down The Alien From Another Dimension, or whatever JFK called him/her/it. His thoughts were a jumble, an unbaked cake of ideas and concepts, some of which were focussed on Miss Happy Lemon Washington but others on something else...a nagging feeling he'd been unable to get rid of since the previous night.

"What *am* I missing?"

~~There is something here in your brain...on the edge... moving around the outskirts.~~

"Can you see it?" Porter asked himself as he reached out to push a large iron door near the school gates. It moved with a loud squeaky creak, the sound of metal and rust and ice being torn apart after an uneasy collaboration. The sound echoed in the playground and made Porter grit his teeth. He hated horrible noises including (but not limited to) drills, rusty doors, screams, and Simon Cowell's dreary speaking voice.

*

Porter was only a few metres away from the silver bike shed when Kitty and Princess Jasmine of Planet Pound caught up with him. He had expected Kitty to follow him out of class, but Porter was surprised to find Jasmine standing alongside her. As little as he knew, they were mortal enemies; Holmes and Moriarty, Doctor Who and The Master, Adam Adamant and The Face, Captain Scarlet and The Mysterons: all had nothing on Kitty Stomp and Princess Jasmine of Planet Pound.

"What are you doing here?" Porter asked Jasmine.

He was unable to mask the suspicion in his tone.

"I am not being left in class by myself. What if our teacher is the weirdo serial killer?"

"That's actually a good point," Porter admitted.

Jasmine glared at Kitty with a glowing look of triumph on her face.

Well, it was either a glowing look of triumph or too much Max Factor.

Porter pushed open the door of the bike shed.

*

JFK was nowhere to be seen.

Instead there was blood; lots and lots of blood.

ALIEN BABYLON

Porter stopped the girls from entering the shed.

"The Alien knew where to find JFK," he told Kitty, "because he had already been here."

"Does it know where *I* live?" Kitty asked quietly, trying not to let Jasmine hear a word.

"No, but it certainly knows where *I* live!"

"How?"

Porter grimaced at the memory of his birthday, the evening he had witnessed The Alien killing a teenager, the struggle still imprinted on his memory. It was the thing he saw in his dreams at night. He felt incredibly foolish, because he had told The Alien exactly where to find him.

"It's a long story," he admitted.

"I used to come to this bike shed when I smoked," Princess Jasmine remarked as she poked her precious head between Porter and Kitty, separating them. Her natural instincts tended towards nosiness, but she instantly gagged with sickness when she saw the inside of the shed.

"This place is gross."

"*You*'re gross!" Kitty snapped.

"At least I'm not a thief," Jasmine sneered, following it with a laugh.

"Your crummy shop isn't worth stealing from!"

Jasmine slapped Kitty across the face with a hand festooned in chunky gold rings.

The blow sent Kitty spinning, but she got up and exacted revenge on her hated enemy; she smiled, nodded, and sucker-punched Jasmine in the stomach.

Porter could only stand by, horrified, as the two girls started pulling at each other's hair.

"No! Stop it! I don't have time for these shenanigans!"

Kitty would have replied, but she was choking in a tight headlock.

"I mean it! Stop this silliness! JFK is in trouble and there's a loony on the loose..."

Princess Jasmine shrieked as Kitty bit her hand until blood trickled down her wrist.

"Bitch!" Jasmine hissed. "I hate poor people!"

Jasmine yanked Kitty forcefully and dragged her brutally across the pavement by her hair, but Kitty thrashed violently until Jasmine lost her balance and fell over. They yelled lots of insults at each other – about alcoholics, unions, capitalism and cheap ironing boards.

*

As the fight raged, suddenly the truth unfolded neatly in Porter's head, the secret finally unlocked.

He caught his breath as it became clear what he had missed from the start.

It was so obvious that he literally cried out in shock. Porter suddenly remembered...

(One of the struggling figures was a teenager, or possibly a child, indistinct but clearly smaller than the other figure, a taller man.)

~~Are you thinking what I'm thinking?~~

"Of course I am," he said, as Kitty successfully landed a savage kick on Jasmine's bum.

(The teenager's hands were wrapped around the man's throat, as though trying to force him away.)

"I can't believe it! I've had the answer all along. I'm so stupid...and self-absorbed. Why didn't I think of it sooner?"

And Porter's inner voice was just as surprised.

~~I can't believe it. You must be wrong.~~

"I don't think so," Porter said thoughtfully.

*

Porter simply abandoned Kitty and Jasmine, leaving them to their own hair-pulling devices. He walked in a daze past the long, winding bridge towards the hills that dwarfed Castlekrankie. The remains of crop circles caught his eye, as usual, but he staggered past them without seeing anything other than his own thoughts. His memories replayed the strange events he had experienced in Castlekrankie, and he re-evaluated everything he knew.

"It was always there in front of me," he muttered, oblivious to what **was** in front of him.

*

At one point on his journey, Porter passed a riot between the strikers and the police. It was taking place at the remains of what looked like a fun fair or carnival. Without realising it, Porter had stumbled upon Joy Land, which sat at the end of the junction just up from The Factory. The policemen were armed, and suited in riot gear. They looked like soldiers from the future, all shiny and hard in their armour. The effect was topped off by shields and visors, which covered their faces.

"STAND DOWN!" a voice yelled through a megaphone. "STAND DOWN AND YOU WILL NOT BE HURT."

Porter walked in a straight line through the hostility, completely unaffected by the violence and noise. He idly wondered how many of the strikers embroiled in the fight had been experimented on by Professor Wrathorga, and whether they would ever get a good night's sleep again. And then he thought about Officer Hatfield, who had lost his son to The Alien. He was probably somewhere in his armour, fighting against men who would never surrender.

I hope you're alright, Porter thought, as two policemen

struggled with a squirming rioter.

A rock whistled past Porter's head, though he barely noticed.

Someone cried out in pain, others cried in anguish and fury.

The police closed in on the rioters.

But Porter merely kept his hands on his handbag – the proof of his individuality.

~~That's not the reason you carry a handbag,~~ his inner voice said for no apparent reason.

The sly words didn't mean anything to Porter.

Yet.

*

Porter soon found himself outside Beckham Block. He looked up and felt a crushing sense of futility. This, he felt, was how it was to fight the future.

He knew the truth.

He knew who was kidnapping and killing all the teenagers in town.

And it was time to put a stop to it, for good.

CRANKY CALLER

Ma and Pa were gone by the time Porter reached his flat, which pleased him because he couldn't be bothered looking at them. Porter used the stairs to reach the summit, because he didn't want to hear another voice that wasn't the other voice inside his head, so that meant avoiding the elevator. His parents hadn't locked the door, which meant they'd left in a hurry. They were probably out setting up a con, Porter supposed.

Porter took a seat in the kitchen and rested his legs. The kettle, which he had filled as soon as he'd got back inside, boiled quickly and he sat with a mug of tea. The house was peaceful and still, in stark contrast to the riot Porter had just passed through.

~~You know you need to make the call.~~

Porter didn't reply to himself. Words weren't necessary. He simply stood up, walked through to his bedroom, past the large David Tennant poster and his bookshelf, towards his luxury bed, where he found his hidden mobile telephone.

Relief surged through Porter when he saw the phone sitting under his pillow where he'd left it a few nights earlier.

~~Ma and Pa didn't find it. They must not have looked. Too busy conning pensioners and that evil Happy Lemon woman. If looks could kill...her face would be a weapon of mass destruction!~~

"She lost her daughter," Porter said coldly, "and her studio has her hooked on energy pills. I refuse to take pleasure in her downfall."

Then he thought it over, adding an extra remark that he hoped would shut up his second voice:

"That would make me as bad as the monster I'm trying to catch."

~~Then do what you have to do and make the call.~~

Porter dialled the relevant number and waited for a response.

*

"Castlekrankie Police," a staid voice said on the other side. "What is your emergency?"

"I wish to report a case of multiple murder and kidnapping."

Porter hoped his statement would be dramatic enough to get him noticed.

"Who is the victim?" the telephone operator asked. Her voice was unwavering in its dullness. It was rather soothing to the ear in Porter's humble opinion, and he fancied himself as an expert in different voices, what with the extra voice he had inside his own brain.

"Victims," he corrected. "That's why I used the word 'multiple' a few seconds ago. I'm not sure how many victims exactly but I'd say…a lot."

"Do you know the identity of the killer?"

"Oh yes," Porter said cheerily, "it's The Alien."

"The Alien?"

"The Alien From Another Dimension, though that's only what my friend calls it. The Alien is actually human."

"And how does your friend know the name of the killer?"

"Oh," Porter laughed, "how remiss of me. My friend knows because he's a spaceman."

The voice paused at the other side, and in the background several voices talked, but it was fuzzy. *Hurry up! I'll have grey hair by the end of this damn call.* Porter shivered at the thought of having grey hair. He yawned down the receiver, hoping the operator would hear his aggravation. The voice returned from the other side and said:

"I've been warned about you."

~~But have they been warned about me?~~

"Is this part of the government conspiracy?" Porter asked, outraged that the operator knew about him. How could this be? Who was talking about him behind his back?

"You're the crank caller who has been harassing Miss Happy Lemon Washington. We traced your calls to this phone. You are breaking the law by making these frivolous calls. You're in a lot of trouble young man."

~~They don't believe us!~~

"Ha!" Porter cried. "That's nothing compared to the trouble I'm about to cook up!"

Porter jabbed the OFF button and killed the connection. The sun was starting to set, and the flat was gloomy and dark. Porter hadn't turned the lights on yet, because he was deep in his own thoughts, thinking of what to do next. The snow storm outside was by now incredibly powerful, making Porter grateful that his new flat had central heating, which kicked in to warm up his world. And yet he didn't feel the slightest bit cosy. It might have been the snow, which was so thick it obliterated his view from the window, frosting the double glazing with a foggy tint. The outline of The Factory was still visible. Porter found himself lured into staring at it:

Why would anyone fight to keep a job in that godforsaken dump?

~~Because people have their pride and they aren't all related to con artists.~~

"That reminds me....we still have to deal with Ma and Pa later."

~~But what are we doing right now? Alfie and JFK have both vanished.~~

"I'm going to call The Alien and sort this out once and for all."

With that said, Porter looked to his phone again, drawing

his thumb across the screen until a familiar name popped up. He waited for a second, unsure whether or not he would be acknowledged. But for some reason – gut instinct or some inexplicable foreknowledge – Porter knew the right person would hear his call.

He pressed his thumb down on the familiar name and waited for an answer.

*

Almost instantly the telephone started ringing.

Porter looked down at his phone in the palm of his hand, but it wasn't ringing at all.

And yet…he could hear the ringing of a telephone.

Chillingly, Porter realised that the sound was coming from *inside* his house.

It was coming from *inside* his bedroom.

Inside his wardrobe!

FILMED IN REAL ALIEN-O-VISION

It was dark, so Porter had to remind himself not to panic. After all, hadn't he recently survived a night being shot at by soldiers? Hadn't he simply walked through a riot? And of course he had managed to endure a lifetime being locked inside a car by his parents.

~~And it made us the men we are today!~~

The sound of a telephone ringing drew Porter closer and closer to his cupboard. It was as if a call centre had opened up a branch in Narnia, and they were ringing from the magical wardrobe – but they didn't know when to quit.

Porter grabbed the handle and pulled the door open with enough force to dislodge it.

A little red telephone sat on a pile of old graphic novels.

He lifted up the phone and stood dumbstruck. *How could this happen?*

He didn't notice a little arm reach out from underneath his bed…

~~Something isn't right here!~~

Porter was about to respond when something sharp pricked the bottom of his leg.

"Ouch!" he yelped in both shock and pain.

Then his world melted slightly, causing Porter to lurch over onto his bed. He felt hot and queasy, his blood suddenly ablaze. His first instinct was to crawl onto his stomach and pull himself up off the floor. He felt a desperate need to protect his feet from, weirdly, the something under his bed.

"Show yourself!" Porter said as he rolled onto his back. But his voice sounded slurry. He tried to speak again, but his tongue was heavy. It was unlike anything Porter had experienced; his tongue was usually sharp and equipped to unleash a good one-liner.

Something crawled out from beneath the bed.

It stood up and loomed over Porter as he lay on his mattress, woozy and weak.

The Alien's grey face didn't have a mouth, so it couldn't smile, but Porter knew it wanted to smile. And its big black eyes didn't blink as it looked down on its latest victim.

"Hello Porter," the Alien said mournfully, *"I didn't want to do this to you, but I knew as soon as we met that this was going to happen."*

The voice sounded oddly familiar, but Porter's ears roared with the sound of hot, angry blood. Whatever was in him had changed his perception. The Alien's voice was a parody of a child's voice, a horrible, vile whisper.

"What...have...you....done....to....me?" Porter asked raggedly.

The Alien raised a grey hand to show off an empty syringe. It was the sort a diabetic might use, or that a child might endure for a flu shot – or that a Professor might make use of when experimenting on soldiers and other reluctant victims.

"This will stop you running off to the human soldiers or the star pilot. It also helps you see me as I really am. But you already know who I am, don't you, Earthling?"

Then:

"That's why you have to die. But your body will be useful when I take control of it. You're strong, Porter. The Alien doesn't want me anymore. It has decided that you will make a better host body."

The little grey man's entire posture changed; his sagging shoulders made him look like a depressed little alien, someone who had finally come to the realisation that he wasn't good enough for the entity hitching a ride inside his brain.

Porter reached out unsteadily and grasped at the enormous grey alien face.

It dropped away to reveal familiar human features.

~~It's a mask! He's wearing a mask!~~

Porter smiled triumphantly, because he had known all along that his enemy was human.

"The Alien From…Another Dimension…I presume."

The smile soon faded from Porter's face when he realised his enemy was also his friend.

*

The face looked at him in understanding.

"Yes, but I used to be a little boy."

It was Alfie.

And his eyes blazed with bright green fire.

DISSECTING THE ALIEN

Alfie used to be a human boy with a perfect life. That isn't an exaggeration; it really was the perfect life, full of happiness and the promise of a good future. He had loving parents and friends, comfort and stability. His loving parents were happy too. They both had good jobs and laughter was the soundtrack to every night at home, when they sat around the dinner table. Yes, they actually had a proper dinner table at which they would sit and eat and talk. The world made sense to him. Alfie's favourite memories of his life were of those times. He remembered the dinner table and his parents in love.

And then everything went to hell.

Hell, for Alfie, was life after The Great Strike of Castlekrankie.

*

They sat in front of the television, eating something resembling pasta. It was welded to their plates with burned cheese. Alfie looked over at his mother and opened his mouth to say something, and then he thought better of it, instead forcing a mouthful of dinner down his throat. It looked like crusty uncooked shells in barely stirred sauce.

"Enjoying it?" Alfie's mother said without looking at him.

She didn't look at him much these days.

"It's really nice, Mum. Thanks."

He pretended to eat what was on the plate but he couldn't.

So instead he asked a question:

"Have you heard from Dad?"

She pretended not to hear her son.

In all honesty she hadn't heard from Alfie's father since the day he'd crossed the picket line and hadn't returned.

That had been over four months ago.

And The Strike was getting nastier and more brutal. No-one could understand or explain why some of the workers had suddenly become more ferocious in their assaults against the police and the scabs. No-one wanted to understand or explain.

People at school had turned on Alfie too because his father had 'broken the picket line'...whatever that meant. Alfie just wanted to see him, so they could sit around the dinner table as a real family once again.

*

One night Alfie decided to go out and find his father.

He put on his tracksuit and trainers, and crept past his sleeping mother, who lay drunk on the living room couch. He simply opened the door and went out.

The Spirit of the Elevator, the annoying Artificial Intelligence that controlled the lift in Beckham Block, decided to taunt him as soon as he reached up to press the button for Ground Floor.

This is a late hour for you to be sneaking out. Get to your bed!

Alfie rolled his eyes and explained himself:

"I can't go back to bed until I find my dad."

You'll never find your dad! He did the right thing by running away. I would run if I had legs.

Alfie was shocked by the savage cruelty of the elevator. But he quickly covered his ears and kept them sheltered from the synthetic voice until the double doors opened, letting him flee with tears pouring down his face.

Have a nice night! The Spirit of the Elevator said conceitedly – or at least with a good interpretation of arrogance.

*

Alfie didn't find his father that night or any other night.

But he did find someone else:

Alfie was out late in the forest when he stumbled on an old man in a white lab coat. For some reason the old man needed help with a large black bag. Alfie smiled and helped him. The old man was a scientist, and he reminded Alfie of his granddad, because he had a bushy white beard and money. He had lots and lots of money! The Professor promised to pay Alfie if he would sit through some medical tests, and Alfie knew his mother needed the money. She had spent her meagre savings on bottles of wine, and the cupboards were completely empty. The pain of losing his father, the constant heartache, was now coupled with hunger pains.

Alfie had to find a way to make money to please his mother.

"Will the medical tests hurt?" Alfie asked, as the wind whipped through the trees.

"No!" The Professor said firmly. "Do I look like a man who would hurt a child?"

Alfie giggled, though the old man didn't understand the joke.

"You look like my grandfather!" Alfie eventually admitted

The Professor smiled compassionately, showing off perfectly white (and false) teeth.

But Alfie felt a sudden chill when he looked up into the eyes of The Professor.

For a moment, just a fraction of a second, he thought The Professor had green eyes.

*

The Professor had lied to him.

The experiments hurt. They hurt so badly that Alfie couldn't even scream.

He looked around to see men strapped onto beds. But not all of them were soldiers: some of them were like his dad, men from The Factory, looking for money.

And some of them were teenagers from school.

*

"How well do you sleep?" The Professor asked during one routine test.

Alfie had come to dread these routine tests, because they involved needles going into his back and fire pouring through his brain and bones.

"I...sleep...." Alfie gasped.

"And do you have bad dreams?"

The answer to this question seemed to fascinate The Professor most of all.

"Yes," Alfie replied, and he was telling the truth. Every single night he dreamed that his dad would never come back home. The Professor didn't reply as he jabbed a cold needle deep into Alfie's neck. Alfie gasped as stinking green liquid drained into him.

"Tell me if this makes the bad dreams better or worse."

"How do *you* sleep at night?" Alfie asked, his brain drowning in chemicals.

"I shut my eyes," The Professor said immediately.

Then his face split open to reveal dripping, squirming green tentacles.

*

Alfie lay on the burst mattress that he called a bed, looking out of the window at the top of Beckham Block, but he did not sleep. He closed his eyes to relax his body, but sleep was always impossible. Sleep was something he remembered doing a long time ago.

Sleep was a distant memory.

The monster inside The Professor's head called itself The Alien From Another Dimension. The Professor wasn't in control of his actions; he had no idea that he was a vessel for a mighty intelligence from the stars. It was The Alien who made him go too far with his experiments. The Professor was nothing but a living puppet, guided by the will of the thing curled up inside his brain.

It lived in dreams, but it wanted to be human.

The Alien From Another Dimension needed more people. It had to have more!

I will walk this world in my own body and crush the life out of these Earthlings with my bare hands.

"Are you real?" Alfie asked The Alien.

I am the nightmare he couldn't drive out of your head. The others can see me too, but they're in a coma, useless and weak. You will be my new servant. But there's something you must do first.

"What?" Alfie asked. "I'll do anything!"

But he already knew the answer.

*

Killing the old Professor was easy.

Alfie simply picked up a hypodermic needle and thrust it between his eyes.

The Professor tipped over and smashed onto the floor as his latest victim lay strapped to a hospital bed. Alfie felt vicious excitement course through him like the chemicals The Professor had injected, and then he giggled.

The boy on the bed looked over in horror but couldn't say anything.

He had been gagged.

Suddenly The Professor's head exploded in a burst of dazzling emerald light.

A corona of green poured from his body into Alfie's eyes, filling his mind.

"I was desperate to escape that decrepit body," giggled Alfie, *"This one will do for now."*

If Porter had been in the laboratory the night The Alien From Another Dimension had hopped into Alfie's body, he would have told him that there was no alien inside him. He would have smacked the old Professor over the head with a handbag.

But most of all he would have recognised the boy strapped to the bed.

It was JFK.

DRAGGED LIKE A SACK, WITH HIS BACK ACROSS A CRACK

Alfie dragged Porter down each and every stair that made up the staircase in Beckham Block. Porter couldn't protest because the drugs in his system had coalesced into a very nasty cocktail. Alfie knew Porter was medicated, so by injecting him with whatever was inside the syringe, Alfie ran the risk of killing Porter with an overdose.

But of course that didn't worry him in the least.

Porter tried his hardest to form enough words to threaten – or at least mock – Alfie, but his jaw didn't want to move. This was agony for Porter!

"You…look…like…a little grey…man."

Alfie released Porter's ankle – the same ankle he had jabbed the needle into – so he could kick Porter hard in the shin.

Porter snarled, but he was unable to reach the brat.

And, even if he had been able, hurting him would have been difficult because of his body armour. Porter recognised it immediately as the remains of riot gear; the gloves, boots and arm protectors weren't included, it was only the chest piece, but it provided Alfie with a terrifying ability to withstand a physical assault.

I wonder what happened to the poor policeman who used to own it.

Ah, Porter thought slyly, *so you're still here with me?*

Idiot, his brother said mockingly, I'm always here with you.

*

"How did you know?" Alfie finally asked between floors eight and seven.

He had to lean down close to hear Porter whispering what tipped him off to Alfie:

"That night I saw the man trying to kill the teenage boy…I witnessed it and something wasn't right, but I didn't know… until I saw Kitty and Jasmine fight earlier tonight."

Porter smiled thinly.

"I realised that I had been wrong all along. The man wasn't…trying to kill that boy. He was trying to *get away* from him. When I saw him putting his hands around the teenage boy's throat, he was pushing him *away*, not…throttling him. The boy was the actual attacker, but I didn't realise it…until too late. Then I realised that the shadow I saw at the Toy Shop was familiar, and I recalled walking with you to school…how you moved."

Alfie laughed, but he was actually quite impressed.

"That boy *was* me, and the man was some random striker from The Factory. He was my third victim of the night. I don't remember his name. Names aren't important, only my work matters!"

"You're…torturing those people…you aren't a scientist like the man who…took you."

"But he brought me to the Alien From Another Dimension, who IS me."

That was when Porter noticed a long thin scar running up Alfie's ear to the top of his head. It looked like someone had performed surgery on him very recently.

*

Alfie managed to get Porter to the edge of Beckham Block – around from the entrance, where too many witnesses might see him. After all, he was officially registered as missing. Every now and then he stopped to get his breath back.

"You're heavier than you look!" Alfie hissed.

To punctuate his point, he kicked Porter in the shin again.

And then he did something far worse than simply assault his ex-friend. Something so vile, so awful, that Porter would probably have nightmares about it for the rest of his life:

Alfie pulled Porter across a cracked pavement.

He giggled as Porter lay on his back, drugged and helpless. He could feel the inconsistent pattern of the cracked concrete burning its print into his back, and though it wasn't really burning him, he almost felt the pain. Stepping on cracks was bad enough, but being yanked across them was worse.

~~WE'LL KILL HIM FOR THIS!~~

There Porter lay until Alfie returned in his spaceship.

His 'spaceship' had four wheels.

It was a police car painted silver.

Porter looked up, his eyes the only part of himself he could move, and caught white light moving towards him: the headlights of the car. But there were white, red and blue lights spinning over him, North of Porter.

~~The police lights will draw a lot of attention.~~

I wonder if his victims looked into those lights before he took them away...

~~Ah, that's a good point. Does he really believe he has an alien hiding inside his head?~~

He does indeed. We must join forces to vanquish the insane brat!

"We're going to the Toy Shop so I can dissect your brain. Then you will become my new body. I'm tired of living inside this tiny body. It proved useful getting people to trust me, and I was able to crawl through the small gap in the wire fence at the army base – you discovered it last night after I killed those human soldiers. But I need strength. And you are strong, Porter, but I didn't realise it when I first saw you in that car."

Alfie's face was twisted with insanity and hate...or was it The Alien inside him?

~~There is no alien inside him. He just thinks there is because~~

of the mad scientist.

"We must be one."

Alfie leaned over to pull Porter into the back of his spaceship when something bright flashed past him. It hit the wall with a slight **POP** and bits of brick chipped away. Unfortunately some of the brick dust drifted down onto Porter's face.

~~I'm going to smack that little brat with a cricket bat.~~

Someone is shooting at him. Maybe Officer Hatfield has come to save us?

CRACK!

Alfie disappeared with frightening speed.

Porter lay on the ground, alone and defenceless.

~~You are never alone,~~ a voice said in his ear.

Someone else was out there in the night, waiting for Alfie.

And whoever it was had a gun.

BECKHAM BLOCKED

A second shot ricocheted off a nearby car, which happened to be Ma and Pa's Crapmobile. Porter wanted to cheer happily but he was too out of it. Alfie moved around frantically, trying to locate the source of the attack: the hunter had become prey for another hunter.

"I am The Alien From Another Dimension," Alfie shrieked behind his four-wheel shield. "Surrender to me and I won't use your brain as a football!"

*

Someone opened their window five floors up and yelled:

"Stop that bloody noise down there! Some of us are trying to sleep!"

*

The Alien From Another Dimension – or Alfie – seemed to react oddly to this statement. Porter knew it was the part about 'sleep' that bothered him, his tired eyes behind his unkempt hair would never close long enough to sleep. Whatever The Professor had done to him and the soldiers, they were beyond repair.

Alfie yelled all sorts of vile death threats at the residents of Beckham Block.

Porter pushed himself off the ground, forcing himself to find the strength to sit up. He inhaled cold air, letting it wake him from his druggy stupor. The injection Alfie had hit him with might have been enough to take out a normal person. But Porter knew what it was to be overmedicated. He recovered magnificently. Soon he was on his feet.

And that was the moment Alfie's 'spaceship' on four wheels came to life.

*

Porter whirled around to see an empty car moving jerkily at him. He was taken aback, trying to decide what to do next. It looked as though the car was alive, because he couldn't see anyone behind the wheel.

~~The car isn't empty. Alfie's just too small to see under the steering wheel.~~

"GET OUT OF THE WAY, PORTER!"

Porter looked over to his left to see a friendly figure standing behind the bin shed, someone he hadn't expected to see alive ever again. It was from there that he had shot at Alfie, under cover of red bricks and plastic bins. His spacesuit was torn and bloody, but it was still in one piece, as was its wearer.

~~It's JFK and he's still alive, which is more than can be said for us unless you move!~~

Porter pushed himself out of the path of the rushing car.

It swerved and stopped suddenly.

Porter watched as Alfie climbed out.

"I killed you," Alfie shouted at JFK. "I got you earlier today when you were in your spaceship! How can you be alive? No-one can survive my power."

Alfie had a hypodermic needle in his right hand, and it caught the moonlight with a threatening gleam. He had used the same syringe to incapacitate dozens of victims.

"Please save me from *it*," Alfie suddenly cried, "it makes me do these things."

But then his entire manner transformed instantly:

"I'm going to enjoy cutting both of you open, Earthlings."

*

Porter opened the door of Ma and Pa's crappy car, the prison in which he had spent entire nights whenever he had defied his parents. Alfie's confusion was enough for JFK to swoop in and snatch the boy off his feet, leaving him thrashing and kicking wildly, his voice a hysterical scream. "I'll kill you both," he spat, whilst trying to stab JFK with the needle in his hand. But he never quite managed to make the needle pierce skin.

JFK responded by throwing Alfie into the back of the car.

Porter darted over and slammed the door shut.

The doors locked instantly, the result of there being no handles.

Two feet shot up at the window and struck it with enough force to crack the glass.

"I should have done that," Porter said thoughtfully as the window broke.

JFK aimed his gun and fired it right at Alfie's chest as he climbed out of the car.

The little boy squealed and crumpled onto the ground, his hand releasing the little hypodermic needle that he had held in his left hand. It fell without a sound.

*

"The Alien From Another Dimension is dead," JFK kept repeating, as if in prayer.

But Porter suddenly recalled a small detail he hadn't yet mentioned to JFK:

"He's wearing body armour!"

*

Alfie leapt up and wrapped his hands around JFK's exposed neck. His lips dripped blood, the result of broken teeth from his violent fall. The fight was a ferocious one and JFK wasn't winning. Alfie was pulling JFK into unconsciousness.

Porter made a quick-but-fatal decision.

He bent down and lifted the syringe Alfie had dropped onto the pavement.

And then he plunged it into a line on Alfie's throat, a long bulging vein.

Alfie's glowing green eyes flickered brightly once more then dimmed severely.

It took Porter a few seconds to work out that Alfie couldn't breathe.

"Where is your inhaler?" Porter cried out.

~~His eyes aren't glowing...does that mean that what he injected us with is wearing off?~~

Alfie climbed to his feet, clawing violently at his throat. He was unsteady, as was Porter, but he still managed to walk a few steps before bursting into tears. JFK was back on his feet with a gun in his hand and a look of determination on his face.

"There has been enough killing," Porter protested.

JFK kept his aim right on his target.

The Alien From Another Dimension turned and spoke using Alfie's burst lips:

"What is happening to me? I...I...can't breathe! I am not human. I cannot die!"

"Where is your inhaler?" Porter repeated. "I'll get it for you!"

Then Alfie laughed. It sounded like a coughing fit.

He knew something they didn't know.

"It doesn't matter. I suppose I'll finally get a good night's sleep."

Alfie spat thick gooey blood.

Then he fell over and died.

*

Sirens in the distance didn't stay in the distance for long.

JFK looked over to see several police cars converging on Beckham Block.

"Someone must have complained about the noise," he said casually to Porter.

Officer Hatfield was first on the scene.

"Porter!" he called out. "What happened here?"

Then he noticed JFK and his face went ashen.

"John?" he gasped. "It's you!"

"Ah," Porter chuckled, "your name is John too."

JFK didn't know what to say and he didn't know what to do, especially when Officer Robert Hatfield swept him up in a tight bear hug.

He had finally found his son.

At last!

*

"A nice happy ending and at least there will be no more death," Porter vowed as he limped in the direction of his flat.

But he couldn't have been more wrong.

Two more people would die very soon.

JOURNEY TO THE CENTRE
OF PORTER MINTER

Porter didn't spend long in his flat before realising he had to go to hospital. He had never stayed overnight at an actual hospital before, because his parents had refused to allow it. The Toy Shop's hospital wing was about as close as he had come to a proper medical facility. Officer Hatfield warned him he had been injected with a very nasty chemical substance, and so he had to go to Castlekrankie Infirmary.

*

Tests were run and it didn't take long for Porter to feel like a human pin cushion, but the tests were necessary to determine what had been done to him. As Porter lay in hospital, he waited for an explanation of the weirdness he had experienced. There had to be an explanation as to why he'd seen the strange things he had whilst under the influence.

It turned out that there was.

The nice doctor explained to Porter that he was full of DMT, or Dimethyltryplamine. It was a drug that induced hallucinations, a powerful alternate state, and there were also traces of a sedative in the compound.

And that's how he managed to kidnap his victims, a voice said in Porter's ear.

"At least I know you aren't an illusion," Porter replied.

No. I'm your brother.

Ma and Pa never once visited Porter whilst he recuperated from his ordeal, a fact he found absolutely intolerable. He sat in bed, going bonkers with boredom. His parents, he knew, were absolute scum, but a part of him still ached at their snub. He couldn't explain why he felt so depressed. His long bouts of seething fury were alleviated by visits from Kitty, who stole grapes from the other patients. They were part of his five-a-year fruit intake.

"How is The Strike?" Porter asked one day.

"It's getting worse. The strikers are killing people. Wrathorga's legacy is now spreading throughout Castlekrankie. Men who can't sleep count bodies instead of sheep."

She looked down at her feet before adding:

"I wonder if my dad underwent one of Wrathorga's 'medical trials.'"

Porter took a grape from her pile and popped it into his mouth.

"The soldiers have disappeared from the Toy Shop. The sleepers have all vanished too."

"You shouldn't have gone back!" Porter chastised gently. "What if they'd shot you?"

"I took a risk and it paid off. The entire Toy Shop has been cleared out, including the infirmary and the secret laboratory. It's all gone."

"Do you know why?" Porter asked grimly. He then paused for dramatic effect:

"It's a government conspiracy!"

Kitty laughed at the irony of Porter stealing her joke.

*

Porter returned to a near-empty home. He bypassed the elevator in favour of the staircase and by the time he got through the front door, he was drenched in sweat. *Goodness, I'm so unfit!* That was his first thought upon realising he was exhausted.

His second thought, however, was:

I would kill for a box of chocolates right now.

Ah...Porter...there's something different about the flat. Can you see it?

He did indeed notice the difference, because everything was packed up into suitcases. The furniture had all but disappeared save a single double couch. The television was gone, as were all the fittings and lampshades. Porter suddenly grabbed the hallway cupboard door handle and pulled it to reveal an empty cupboard.

The suitcase containing his brother was missing!

Porter forgot his fatigue and ran into his bedroom. It was still the same, completely untouched by the interfering hands of his parents. They had packed away everything except for his stuff. A harsh understanding dawned on Porter.

"They're planning to leave me!"

But isn't that what we both want? We can finally get away from them!

Before Porter could tell his other voice to shut up, he heard the familiar sounds of his parents returning home. He waited in his room, listening to what they were talking about, which wasn't difficult because they were so obnoxiously loud.

"He's isn't due to leave for another day, so we have the flat for tonight."

"Where shall we go next, my dear?" This was Ma. Porter gritted his teeth in anger.

"We can go anywhere, my temptress, because Unhappy Lemon Washington has cut us a cheque that will keep us in the standard of living to which we've become accustomed!"

The sound of evil laughter came from the empty kitchen.

"That stupid cow really thinks we'll bring her daughter back from a UFO!" Pa chortled.

"We have to leave soon – before the press breaks the story of that horrid little boy."

There was a slice of silence that suggested someone didn't know what to say. And then Pa spoke up, because he wanted his wife to clarify something for him:

"Are you referring to the insane killer child or our ungrateful son?"

Porter opened his cupboard, retrieved one of his handbags, and walked out of his room with a purposeful stride. It was only when he had left his room that he noticed his parents hadn't packed everything away.

The old lawnmower sat at the far end of the hallway.

*

Porter did something completely insane.

He turned the key on the lawnmower and let it loose.

*

Ma screamed as the lawnmower smashed aimlessly through the wall, chomping at plaster and wood, slicing and dicing any solid barriers that stood between her and Porter. Pa yelled in fright and actually pushed his wife in front of him, so she would be eviscerated first. They both cried out in terror, trying their best to flee the deadly mower.

Unfortunately for Porter, the lawnmower ran out of precious custard fuel and spluttered to a full halt inches away from his hateful parents.

"You are an absolute fiend from the depths of hell!" Pa said with wide eyes.

"We're getting away from you," Ma screamed, "we're going to get away tomorrow. You can't stop us! Let's see how you live without our money to support you!"

"It is not *your* money," Porter retorted. "It's money from your victims."

"Money you'll never see!" Ma said between deep breaths. Porter thought mistakenly that he'd induced a heart attack in his mother, but alas she was able to bring her breathing under control and soon returned to her normal ghastly self.

"You won't survive without us and the wealth we provide."

But she was wrong. Porter knew all about survival.
And death.

MY PIZZA PARENTS

Porter's plan to do away with his parents wasn't especially complicated. Indeed it was only a matter of making a few phone calls to certain people. The only problem was timing. Whatever! His parents wouldn't be around for much longer either way.

*

It took a good hour to revitalise his mobile telephone, which had been weakened from overuse. Porter plugged it into a plug socket in his bedroom while he set about the important task of plotting his revenge. The first thing he did was go online to search for the contact details of certain people.

Porter sat in front of a screen for hours. He stifled a yawn and ventured out of his room for tea and toilet breaks. He typed names into the search engine, before adding the specific town in which the individual lived.

Making telephone calls in secret was a bit difficult, but Porter managed to keep his voice low. And where he couldn't find someone, he simply sent them a text message or email.

~~What are you doing?~~

"You know what I'm doing because you are inside my head."

~~Will you finally free me from the darkness of the suitcase?~~

"Yes."

*

The next morning started with Porter feeling a stifling mixture of excitement and anxiety. He couldn't quite work out which was more overpowering. The weather had also changed, as an added bonus for his plans; for the first time in months the snow was chased away by gorgeous humid sun. Porter wanted to remain in bed, with the quilt snugly wrapped around him – but he had to be awake to make sure his plan worked.

His plan was murder.

*

"You'll need to go to the food bank later today," Ma said to him as he entered the kitchen to make himself breakfast. But breakfast was impossible, for the cupboards were completely emptied out. Not even a can of custard was left. Ma and Pa were trying to prove a point, of course.

Porter smiled but didn't reply.

He desperately hoped his plan would work.

"The House of Chicken will give you all the food you need. After all…it's their job to help the poor!" Pa laughed.

The smile didn't leave Porter's face, not for a second.

*

The mob arrived at eleven o'clock.

Porter actually heard them before he saw them. But the noise from the crowd below told him that not only had his plan worked, it had worked better than he could have imagined. He jumped off his bed and ran over to the window, peering down from on high to see the source of the commotion. He already knew, of course, and realised that his neighbours had probably caught a similar view a few nights prior when he had taken on The Alien, together with JFK.

"What is that noise?" Pa's voice came easily from the living room where his luggage was waiting for him. "Is it something to do with that damn Factory again? I'm sick of those filthy begging tramps trying to get their jobs back. Just give it up!"

Porter clapped his hands happily at the sight of the rabble.

It was all he could do to keep gleeful words inside his throat, buried away from his parents; words of warning: boastful words that revealed his genius in the art of war.

Those in the crowd were walking down the street, bearing an array of blunt implements including (but not limited to) golf clubs, baseball bats and hammers. One of the mob, a pensioner who shuffled slightly behind the gang, clutched a canister of oxygen to which a mask on her face was hooked. She swung it angrily in time with the rest of the pack's weaponry.

There was only one problem with the plan.

Beckham Block was a private residential estate, albeit a very tall one, which meant his parents were secure as long as no-one let them into the building.

*

Porter quietly tip-toed out of his bedroom and opened the downstairs door.

And then he waited for his revenge to be delivered.

*

It was only when one of the group – a six-foot-tall man who looked like a wrestler – kicked open the front door that Ma and Pa Minter knew the jig was up. Porter hid in the hallway cupboard, watching the events from between a crack in the door, and loving every second of them.

There were at least two dozen people in the crowd.

Each one of them was a victim of the Minters in some capacity. They had either been conned out of money or were connected to someone who had been conned out of money.

"No!" Ma threw her hands up in protest. "You've got the wrong people!"

Pa, however, made no pretence of his fear at what was about to happen to him.

"How did you find us?" he asked tearfully.

"Please don't hurt me!" Ma screamed in terror as she was overwhelmed by the sheer force of numbers in the crowd. "It wasn't me, I swear! My husband made me steal from you!"

Porter couldn't see a lot of the actual violence, which was just as well because he was somewhat squeamish when it came to blood and guts. But he heard the sounds of punches being thrown, clubs being swung, and most of all he heard his parents screaming as they were battered senseless. A part of him felt pangs of guilt, and he even thought about rescuing his parents…but the other part – the piece of him that he carried from his brother, the boy in the suitcase – willed the violence onto ludicrous extremes.

~~They deserve it, Porter. Surely you see that they both deserve it?~~

Then bitterly the voice added:

~~They killed me.~~

When Porter left the safety of the cupboard, no-one questioned his presence because he could have been part of their group. Why? Because of all of Ma and Pa's victims, none had suffered quite as badly as he – their son – had.

"I say we take them both up to the roof," he declared as he retrieved his handbag from the bedroom. "Beckham Block is one of the tallest buildings in town."

The words tumbled out of his mouth before he could even think them through.

It was going to look like a suicide, which was the whole point.

*

Porter let the cold wind sweep his dark hair across his eyes, a wild gust full of strength and warmth. The typical chill of Castlekrankie was now a bracing and beautiful breeze. He breathed in the air and felt, without warning, a burst of dizziness overwhelm him.

"I'm nearly as tall as The Factory," he said, his eyes focussing on the black chimneys in front of him. He had to focus on that specific building in order to steady himself.

The gang were already at the edge of the room, dragging Ma and Pa along the ground, spitting on them, glorying in their victory. Porter heard snatches of stories, words that danced on the wind: pregnant women left with no money to pay their rent, families breaking up, suicides, and self-loathing.

Ma shouted something at Porter.

The wind whipped up into a powerful burst.

Then his parents went over the edge and all the way down.

Farewell forever.

Or to be more succinct…SPLAT!

MEMORANDUM

to:	The Prime Minster
from:	Sir Hemmingford Higginson
subject:	The Experiment

The experiment has been abandoned but it was not a complete disaster.

The Sleepers will need to be killed off as a precaution. The Professor couldn't cure their Post Traumatic Stress, but his work yielded interesting results.

The men and women experimented on by The Professor exhibited signs of increased aggression, and a penchant for extreme violence. Castlekrankie was a good place for our tests. The industrial strike provided excellent cover because people blamed the incidents of violence on the strikers. The child who had tests conducted on him by The Professor was a random element, but he is no longer a threat now that he's dead.

If we could take what The Professor did to The Sleepers and apply it to our men, then we could conceivably have a new weapon to use against our enemies. We could increase the savagery of our armed forces and turn them into an unstoppable force.

We will go elsewhere. We will not be found. Our work will continue.

THE SECRET IN THE SUITCASE

Porter was in the remains of his flat when Kitty appeared with bags of food.

"I liberated these from the local corner shop," she said with a smile. Her veil was completely gone, and she no longer wore black but, instead, a nice angora sweater of the fluffiest red and green. Her hair was almost a complete crop, but it suited her. In her other hand was a copy of the *Castlekrankie Chronicle*, which Porter had requested.

"So JFK was actually on his way to a fancy dress party when The Professor got him, and that was the night he met Alfie?"

"Yes," Porter explained patiently as Kitty listened.

"And he was dressed as an astronaut. Does that explain the delusion?"

"I'm not sure, to be honest. Professor Wrathorga definitely messed with his head."

Kitty nodded, completely at ease with Porter's opinion.

"What did the police say about your parents?" she asked as Porter rifled through the paper bag for some snacks. He found a large bag of salt and vinegar crisps, which he eagerly pounced on.

"Nothing of any consequence," he admitted between crunches. "In fact they seemed a bit uninterested, which is just the way I like it."

Truth be told, Porter had been petrified they would find his brother inside the suitcase he now had in front of him. But the death of his parents was sure to be ruled as a suicide. ~~Thank goodness,~~ a voice said in Porter's left ear.

But there was something else troubling Porter.

"Ma shouted just before she...fell."

"What did she say?"

"She said...'He isn't in the suitcase.'"

"He isn't in the suitcase?"

Kitty didn't understand what that meant.

Porter reached over to the suitcase and gripped onto the clasps beside the handle. They had once been gold, but the colour had all but scraped off to reveal a bronze derivative. His heart pounding, echoing up until his hands trembled, Porter knew it was time to do something he hadn't done since he'd been a child.

He opened up the suitcase.

*

There was no body inside it.

There were only documents and papers and photographs.

Porter groaned loudly, his dismay obvious to Kitty.

"I saw him! I saw him! It wasn't my imagination!"

Kitty backed away as her friend started head-butting his knees in trauma.

He suddenly stopped as quickly as he had started.

Then he went through the photographs.

They revealed something quite startling.

*

In each photograph were his parents. Ma and Pa looked slightly different in each shot, but they were still recognisably his parents. But they weren't alone in them:

In each photograph they had a different child alongside them.

And although each child looked completely different, they all had one thing in common.

They all had the same face as Porter.

Kitty lifted one photograph and studied it carefully.

"They're you, Porter. But...you look completely different in all of them."

"I can't remember being in *any* of these photos."

But there was another surprise to come.

There was even one photograph in which Ma and Pa stood hand in hand with a girl between them. She wore a little blue and white dress, and clutched a modest Barbie doll.

"Porter…" Kitty said slowly, deliberately choosing her words so she didn't offend her friend. "They've dressed you as a girl in this photograph."

The documents in the case were old and wrinkled, but each piece of paper was a different birth certificate. Porter frantically went through them all, realising quickly that each was marked with *his* birthday.

"How many people have you been?" Kitty asked sadly.

"I don't remember being *any* of these people!"

~~Is it any wonder we took a nervous breakdown?~~

"They've spent years building me up, making me into different people. How many different versions of me have they killed off? I think one of my previous personalities eventually broke through. But I swear I had a brother, and they killed him. I saw him in the suitcase. I did!"

And the memories suddenly burst through Porter's mental defences, bombarding him with more than just a voice; names, people, places flashed clearly and concisely…

*

I am Gerry, I am Kyle, I am Derrick, I am Martin, I am Michael, I am Ralph…yes can you believe they called me Ralph…I am Becky, I am Iwen, I am so many different people, can you remember us now? We were you and you were us. **Now you are Porter Minter,** the boy with the handbag and the will to win. But is that really your handbag or is Becky choosing them? She always liked a good handbag. *Do you remember us, Porter? Do you? Your brother is the loudest but we all speak to you in our own little ways.*

*

They found one photograph that revealed an older boy standing beside Porter as a child, hugging him protectively. But Porter couldn't remember if this was his brother. His past was a flimsy tapestry of truths, half-truths, and downright lies.

The suitcase contained more than just photographs.

There was also a life insurance document.

Porter nearly tipped over when he realised that he would now be the recipient of an enormous amount of money.

He laughed and didn't stop until Kitty slapped him. She enjoyed it slightly.

But there was one last question to answer.

*

"What did Alfie do with all the bodies?" Kitty asked, as Porter picked up the newspaper. He was interested in the headlines, because he wanted to see what the reporters had written about his battle with Alfie – or The Alien, as he called himself.

But there was absolutely nothing, not even a hero's welcome for Porter.

The main story was about the anonymous food donations

to the House of Chicken.

"I mean you can't just hide a dead body. There has to be a trace of it somewhere. Alfie, and The Professor before him, bumped off loads of people. So where are they?"

Porter was too busy reading about the succulent chicken that had the people of Castlekrankie queuing out the food bank for hours. The Factory, it turned out, had also been a beneficiary of this mysterious food philanthropist's generosity. The succulent Marlowe Meat Pies were being filled with the same succulent chicken that this new supplier was providing.

"There have to be traces of these people *somewhere*!" Kitty said loudly.

That was when Porter suddenly understood the sickening truth.

He dropped the newspaper.

~~Oh dear.~~

"What is it Porter? Are you alright? You suddenly look a bit pale."

The Marlowe Meat Pie slogan was included on the newspaper page in an advert that was clearly some form of damage control against the strikers.

OUR PIES, OUR PEOPLE: Made From Real Meat Juices!

Porter placed his hands across his mouth to stop the words (and vomit) tumbling out.

"I'm okay," he finally said, "I'm vegetarian."

"What are you on about? *I'm* not vegetarian."

"Do you remember when we were trapped in the Toy Shop," Porter started, slowly getting to the point, "when we discovered Wrathorga's secret lab?"

"Do I remember?" Kitty laughed sarcastically. "I'm trying to forget it!"

"You mentioned Burke and Hare…"

"Oh! Yes. The Scottish serial killers who murdered people and sold their bodies to a scientist for medical research. I thought that was what Professor Wrathorga had been doing to our classmates."

Porter didn't quite know how to put the next bit into words.

"Do you know who Sweeney Todd was?" Porter asked her offhandedly.

Kitty perked up.

"Oh yes! I've got a copy of the musical soundtrack somewhere in my collection of stuff. I might have pinched it from my sister. Sweeney Todd murdered people, and he got his accomplice to dispose of their bodies. She's a pie maker and they're in love..."

Kitty stopped. She slowly looked down at the advert in the newspaper again.

OUR PIES, OUR PEOPLE: Made From Real Meat Juices!

"He wouldn't. He couldn't!" she gasped, but she looked very doubtful.

Porter scrunched up the newspaper and violently hurled it across the room.

"Don't eat anything from The House of Chicken and don't buy a Marlowe Meat Pie."

"I'm a vegetarian now," Kitty said before running off to the toilet to be sick.

EPILOGUE
GOODBYE CASTLEKRANKIE

Porter watched the town from inside the relative sanity of the bus. It was the X39 that picked him and his handbag up first, so he went with it. Anywhere was better than Castlekrankie. He didn't know where he would go, but his bank account was full of numbers – impossible numbers – on which he could easily live for the rest of his life. He also had dozens of passports, each bearing a different version of his face. He could easily survive for years to come under dozens of aliases.

No-one would find him.

~~What will we do without Ma and Pa?~~

"Live a normal life," Porter told himself, much to the hilarity of his fellow passengers.

The bus turned up a lane and moved swiftly down the road, past the food bank. Porter gave it a cursory glance. The queue outside was enormous and his stomach threatened to betray him and rinse out on the bus. But much to his surprise he recognised someone in the queue.

Princess Jasmine of Planet Pound was waiting with a slightly furtive expression on her face and a plate in her hands. She was flanked by a tired-looking man and presumably his wife, whose hand he held tightly in his own. Jasmine's parents must have fallen hard if they too needed the food bank.

The food bank was busy, Porter noticed. So exceedingly busy in fact that it would probably have to move to larger premises.

~~Shouldn't we tell everyone the truth?~~

"Let the fools find out for themselves," Porter said bitterly.

The bus trembled slightly but it wasn't because of a sudden

turn or a large pot hole. Porter turned to his right and watched as the skyline of Castlekrankie changed irrevocably. At first he didn't understand why there was a fire in the sky, but it soon became apparent that something had just unleashed a shockwave so mighty that even the bus had felt it keenly.

Then Porter realised what had changed:

The Factory was on fire. The shockwave had been an explosion.

Black smoke was soon followed by the dramatic sight of collapsing chimneys. The demolition transformed the horizon. The X39 moved past dark-eyed strikers, who celebrated their victory with a sumptuous feast of pie – the same delicacy they had once baked for a living.

~~We need to get the hell out of...hell.~~

"Shut up!" Porter admonished himself, much to the astonishment of the other passengers. "We're leaving this rotten dump. Don't ask me where we're going. I have no idea. But it won't be as bad as this horrid carbuncle of a town."

Porter had a map in front of him, sitting on his lap, a tool his parents had used when travelling across the country, selecting their next victims. It was creased from overuse. Porter really had no idea where he would go next. But he knew it would be a new start. A brand new life in a brand new town! It would be a wonderful place full of quaint architecture and classy people who refused to eat pies or custard.

Porter closed his eyes and jabbed his index finger down on the rumpled paper.

THE END

HELLO YOU!

If you're reading this page, chances are you've finished *North Of Porter,* in which case I really hope you enjoyed it. If you haven't finished it, WHY ARE YOU READING THIS? You've started my book the wrong way around! Start at the other end, you fool!

When I told people I was writing a book about a handbag-wielding boy battling a serial killer in a weird town, they automatically assumed it was my autobiography. It's not – I've never battled a serial killer. (A strange man did once leap out from a bush when I was walking through a Tesco car park, but he turned out to be my long lost dad.)

If you've liked what you've read, delve into my world of oddness. Follow me on Twitter. Follow me on Facebook and Instagram.

But don't follow me home!

www.KirklandCiccone.com
www.Twitter.com/KirklandCiccone
www.Instagram.com/KirklandCiccone
www.Facebook.com/ConjuringTheCiccone
http://omgkirklandciccone.tumblr.com

Kirkland Ciccone AKA Kirkotron 5000